Aaron Steele had stirred up something inside her that no man had done before.

The feelings Bethany experienced that night when she returned to her hotel room were confusing. Though the only physical contact they had was when he touched her arm, he had made her feel passion— the desperate need for restraint. And it wasn't because he was a famous and romantic actor. Had he been an accountant it would be the same. The fact remained that Aaron Steele was a man—all man. Well over six feet of desirable male that she suddenly longed for.  ould know the strength his whis- pered word his lips on hers.

She drop ing in her eyes. "Oh, ay is this happening to me? Help me control it, for these feelings are new to me! Dear Lord, please—I pray that I may not have the opportunity to have to decide what to do. But if the temptations do come, help me resist this man!"

BORN TO BE ONE

Cathie LeNoir

Serenade/Serenata
BOOKS
of the Zondervan Publishing House
Grand Rapids, Michigan

Serenade/Serenata is an imprint of
The Zondervan Publishing House
1415 Lake Drive, S.E.
Grand Rapids, Michigan 49506

ISBN 0-310-47062-5

Printed in the United States of America

85 86 87 88 89 90 / 10 9 8 7 6 5 4 3 2 1

To God be the glory

CHAPTER 1

BETHANY WAS STRUGGLING between elusive fantasies and reality. It was difficult to believe that it had actually happened, yet here she was, in Los Angeles, tasting the first fruits of success.

She wandered to the window of her hotel room, looked out at the blinking lights of the city, and smiled at her own astonishment. This was so typical, she thought. For a long time you keep asking God for something and when He finally grants your request, you act surprised! What kind of faith is that?

She chuckled softly. How patient God must be with me, she mused. How understanding and loving and— the list was endless.

She opened her two suitcases and began unpacking the clothes she brought along, hanging the blouses and dresses and pants in the closet and setting the lingerie and sweaters in a neat little pile to be placed in drawers.

She had brought a variety of things to wear, not

quite certain of how the weather would be in January in the "sunshine state." When she left Denver, the snow was deep and the air brisk, typical conditions for the Rocky Mountain states. But it was surprising to step outside the Los Angeles airport upon her arrival and shiver at the cold, damp air. The taxi driver, who transported her to the hotel, told her it was because of the humidity. It was probably a good thing she brought along some warm sweaters.

At the bottom of one suitcase were two books. One was her Bible, which she lovingly placed on the small table next to her bed. The other was a brand new leather bound Thesaurus. She opened it and reread the inscription inside: *"To our dear Bethany: our successful writer! May your gifted pen always glorify God! Love, Mom and Dad."*

She held the book a moment, tender thoughts of her parents going through her mind. They had always been supportive of her writing. Ever since she started.

She remembered the first play she ever wrote when she was only ten years old. The play was a one-act, so-called comedy in which the players (all neighborhood children) were chickens, complaining about having nothing to do but lay eggs. The play also laid a large egg. It was presented in Bethany's back yard and attended by one person, a five-year old boy who had nothing better to do and who even lacked the ten-cent price of admission.

It was a start, though, for Bethany, and it wasn't long before her natural ability surfaced. In high school she wrote several plays, successfully performed by students of the drama classes. When she graduated from high school she began to write plays for the little theater group in her home town near Denver, and the praise from the local papers encouraged her to take a step further. A gigantic step. A play for television.

Bouncing around in her head, for as long as she could remember, was the desire to write about the Apostle John, the author of the fourth gospel, three epistles, and the book of Revelation. Bethany could see much of his character in what he wrote. But she didn't enter into the project without a great deal of prayer and a lengthy discussion with her pastor, who told her that if God wanted the story told on TV, nothing could stop it.

Bethany held in retrospect the last five years of hard work and the disappointments that preceded her success. Endless nights at the library, pondering over books on TV script writing, technique of outlines, breakdowns, and marketing. Then rising in the morning while it was dark and her parents still asleep, and writing. Sometimes. Sometimes staring at a blank piece of paper for hours. Then putting in a full day's work waiting tables at the cafe. Then back to the library at night. No time for many dates, not that there were any young men around that really interested her. Then the bitter disappointment she received in trying to submit her finished work on her own, prompting her to return to the library for a list of agents handling television scripts and then back to the house to write letters to each one on that list, hoping and praying.

Then an established and experienced agent, took an interest in her writing. Calvin Bruce could see her ability as well as her potential, he said in his letters.

And then the breath-taking thrill—that moment when the long-distance phone call came from Calvin, telling her he had found a producer interested in her script.

She finished unpacking and ran a bath. Soaking in the warm water, she thought of the day ahead of her. Tomorrow, she would meet Aaron Steele, the handsome actor who would play John. Her heartbeat increased over the idea. She prayed hard that God would help her speak rationally to the famous actor.

She met her agent for the first time when he picked her up at the hotel at eleven o'clock the following morning. Calvin Bruce was short, balding, in his late forties, and had an infectious grin and eyes that spoke of sincerity. Bethany took an immediate liking to him.

"I thought you would call me from the airport when you got in," he said lightly. "I was surprised when you called this morning and said you were already here! Are you always that independent?"

"Usually," she replied with a smile. "Sometimes to a fault, I think. But I didn't want to bother you at home."

He eyed her shrewdly. "Well, that's very considerate of you, but I'm not a family man. I was divorced five years ago and I live alone." He opened the door to the car for her and she climbed in. "You're younger than you sound on the phone," he remarked.

"I'm twenty-five. It seems like the years are going by fast enough!"

"Wait until you hit forty! That's when a year seems like a day." He drew out a cigarette. "Do you smoke?"

"No. Thank you."

"Mind?" He already had the cigarette between his lips.

"No. That's OK."

"They're meeting us in my office," he said.

"They?"

"Mike Innes, the producer, and Aaron Steele. Aaron really fell in love with the part. Think he'll do it justice?"

Bethany felt a fluttering sensation at the mention of the actor's name. She had seen Aaron Steele in several motion pictures and numerous TV shows. He was an accomplished actor. Physically she could picture him as the Apostle John, but so many of his films had been filled with violence, it was difficult to imagine the seemingly egotistical and arrogant actor as the earnest and devoted John—the "disciple whom Jesus loved." Yet, Aaron Steele was a marvelous actor. And she had to remember, God was in charge.

"I'm pleased that he liked it so well," she said. "And yes, I–I'm sure he'll do just fine."

They waited for over an hour for the actor and the producer to arrive. While Calvin excused himself to do some paper work at his desk, Bethany rearranged herself in the comfortable chair and smoothed the skirt of her teal-blue wool suit, wondering if she should have chosen something else to wear for this important meeting. The white silk shirt was neat and simple and went well with the suit, and the teal blue complemented her light brown hair and blue eyes. But maybe she should have "dressed up" a little more. Perhaps the black dress with a strand of pearls—she was pondering over this when the door opened.

"Hi, Cal! You've met Aaron, haven't you?"

Calvin stood up. "Yes, we met once before about six months ago on the set of 'My Partner, My Gun.' "

Aaron Steele extended his hand. "That's right," he said with a flashing smile. As introductions were

11

made, he turned to Bethany, and she felt her limbs grow weak. She was grateful for the chair under her trembling body.

"And this is Bethany—what's the last name?"

"J—uh—Jordan," she stammered, wondering where all her professionalism was. "Bethany Jordan."

"Bethany and Jordan," he quipped. "Your parents must be big on geography!"

Without giving her a chance to respond, he sat down and turned to Calvin again. For all of fifteen minutes the handsome actor graced his audience with the magnificence of his perfectly modulated voice, as he spoke of trivial things—Calvin's secretary and how "sexy" she was; another script he had just read for a TV series that he was considering; how much he hated the cold weather. Throughout the brief conversation, he frequently looked at Bethany. Sometimes he only glanced quickly in her direction, but sometimes his eyes grazed over her body, taking in her shapely legs and causing her to feel both uneasy and excited. Once he caught her eyes and held them, and she nervously licked her dry lips and looked down at the carpet.

Then he stood up. "Well," he said, "Mike has some things to discuss with you, Calvin. I've told him what I want changed in the script. I hope you'll excuse me now. I have a luncheon date. Nice meeting you," he added, with a brief nod at Bethany. Then he was gone.

Bethany stayed in her hotel room that night. She had been asked to cocktails and dinner by Calvin and Mike Innes, but declined. She had no desire to sip cocktails, first of all, and secondly, after that meeting, she had much to pray about.

Already they wanted to change things, she thought sourly. The title, for starters.

"I just don't think 'Agape, John,' is good, Cal," Mike had said. "No one will know what 'agape' means. We have to come up with something else."

And so it went. While she sat, almost unnoticed, the two of them hashed over her script, discussing the changes that Aaron Steele had requested. The actor didn't feel comfortable leaning against Jesus at the Last Supper. He didn't feel reference to the name Salome, mother of John, should be given, because the audience might confuse that Salome with the daughter of Herodias, who danced before Herod and earned the head of John the Baptist. He objected to the character change in John. Since John and his brother James were called "Sons of Thunder" by Jesus, he had asked, then why was this vehemency so conspicuously absent toward the end of the play?

As the producer rattled on, Calvin had glanced now and then to Bethany, communicating apologies and also the necessity to rewrite. Mike Innes occasionally turned to her and asked what she thought, but before she could voice her opinion, he would go on with something else. She had no chance to discuss anything with Calvin alone as yet, but perhaps that was just as well. She needed time to pray about it first.

With a heavy heart she climbed into bed, held her Bible, and closed her eyes.

"Dear, sweet Jesus," she began. "I'm so confused. I don't want to change things as you have written them in Your Word just to please the whim of this arrogant actor."

She paused a moment to reflect on Aaron Steele. He obviously must have some knowledge of the Bible, but he apparently knew little of the saving grace of Jesus Christ.

The transformation of the character of the Apostle John was certainly attributed to Jesus. No one but God could bring about such a change in one's personality. Jesus saw John's shortcomings: his impatience, intolerance, and quick temper. But with a love of which only God is capable, the Lord gently and patiently taught and guided, until the Apostle mellowed into the loving character so evident in his later life.

What a shame Aaron Steele couldn't see that!

She sighed. The actor was so handsome! What a pity his personality wasn't as pleasing as his looks! She continued in prayer.

"I feel so much resentment, Lord, that I know I shouldn't be feeling. Please—tell me what to say. Tell me what to do!"

She opened her Bible to Exodus 14:13. She felt the quickening of the Holy Spirit as she read the answer she needed: "Fear not, stand still, and see the salvation of the Lord."

She closed her eyes and smiled. How confident, comforted, and loved Moses must have felt when he heard those words! Just as she felt right now!

"Thank you Lord!" she whispered.

CHAPTER 2

"I'LL HAVE AN EXTRA dry Martini," Calvin said to the waiter.

"And the lady?"

Bethany shook her head. "Nothing, thank you." She hoped Calvin wouldn't pressure her about being a teetotaler, since she noticed most of the people around them were sipping some kind of alcoholic beverage.

As if readying her mind, he said, "Lots of drinking in this city. I guess you noticed that, didn't you?"

Bethany flushed. "It seems so, yes."

"You don't drink?"

"No."

"And you don't smoke?"

"No."

"Hm." He grinned. "Well, I'll omit asking you anything else. That would be too personal!"

The blush in Bethany's cheeks deepened, but Calvin had the graciousness not to comment on it.

"Bethany," he said, "I didn't bring you to lunch to discuss your virtues."

She smiled. "Thanks. That's a relief!"

He laughed, then grew serious. "I would imagine, after yesterday's meeting, that you must have some questions," he said. "And there are a couple of things I have to advise you about." He took a sip of the Martini and smacked his lips. "Um, that's good. Now, as to Aaron Steele—"

She interrupted. "I should hope he doesn't expect me to rewrite the entire script just to suit him!" she said crisply. Then she lowered her eyes. "I'm sorry. I didn't mean to sound pig-headed."

"Good. That's the first thing you have to learn, Bethany. You're a newcomer. Your reputation isn't established as yet."

"My reputation?"

"Um." He sipped the Martini again. "Soon, you'll be introduced to the world of TV script editors. You'll be discussing with them possible changes in the script, budget restrictions, and so forth. Your attitude at those meetings will circulate faster than a speeding bullet."

"What do you mean?"

"I mean, if you are unable to listen, or show signs of being arrogant or belligerent, your reputation will be established as being 'difficult.' You will be labeled as trouble, and your chances of future work will suffer. Now I don't think you are any of those things, Bethany. You seem to me to be patient and cooperative for the most part. And intelligent and quite professional, actually."

"Thank you, Calvin, I appreciate your telling me this."

"Now, honey, I understand how you feel, believe me. You've worked hard at your craft and you like your finished work just the way it is. You've probably already done a lot of rewrite on it and feel that it can't be improved, right?"

"Well . . ." She laughed. "OK, I guess you're right."

"I know I am. All I'm saying is, be flexible. And the next thing I want you to learn, honey, is that you have a right to speak up. If you object to a change, then certainly you may state your feelings. But take care in the way you do this, OK? Don't be too defensive."

"I understand. Thank you, Cal."

He lifted his glass in a toast and winked. "We're gonna make money, Bethany."

She smiled. That was secondary in importance to her. She lifted her water goblet and clinked it against his cocktail glass.

"There's a party tonight in the Valley. Would you like me to take you?"

"Is it important for me to go?"

He paused and thought a moment. "Not as far as your career is concerned. No one will be there that will help you in that respect. But I think you should get acquainted. You'll be here in LA for awhile. I can't see you just sitting alone in your hotel room every night."

"That's very thoughtful of you, Cal. And sometime I will take you up on it. But tonight, I think I'll pass. I have several letters to write."

"OK. There'll be lots of other times. There's always something going on. But call me if you get bored or lonesome won't you?"

"Yes. I will."

"Promise?"
"Promise."

That evening, after Bethany washed her hair, she took a warm, relaxing bath, then put on a robe and turned on her blow dryer. When her hair was almost dry, she sat at the small desk in her room and began to write a letter to her parents, since she knew that the quick telephone call she made to them at the airport certainly didn't satisfy. After that, she would send postcards to her friends back home, as she knew they were all anxious to hear from her.

> Dear Mom and Dad:
> It's been really exciting so far! I met my agent, Calvin Bruce, and he's every bit as nice as he sounded on the phone. He took me to his office where I met the producer and Aaron Steele, the actor who has the lead in my play. Aaron Steele is terribly handsome. . . .

She chewed on the end of her pen a moment, then crumpled the letter, threw it into the waste paper basket and began again. This time she wrote "very nice" instead of "terribly handsome." She didn't want her parents to jump to the conclusion that she had fallen in love with the famous actor at their first meeting. Not that she had, of course! The idea was ridiculous!

Staring pensively at nothing in particular, she reflected on whether or not she was being completely truthful in calling it a ridiculous notion to have fallen in love with Aaron Steele. Then, puzzled because the idea filled her with confusion, she forced herself to dismiss the thought from her mind and concentrate on her letter. She avoided any further mention of the actor, and finished the letter with another complimentary paragraph on Calvin Bruce.

She felt good about the luncheon meeting with Cal. She had been a bit taken back when he started he call her "honey" but she had to get used to that, probably. "Honey" and "darling" were thrown about rather carelessly in this place, it seemed.

She was about to begin writing postcards to her friends when the phone rang and she jumped. Probably Calvin, she thought, worried about her, and she looked to see what time it was. It was eight o'clock.

She lifted the receiver. "Hello?"

"Bethany?"

"Yes." The voice was deep, strangely familiar. "Who is this?"

"It's Aaron."

Her throat went dry. "Aaron Steele?"

"How many Aarons do you know, sweetheart?" He laughed.

She stiffened and said nothing.

"I'm downstairs. May I come up?"

"No!" she shrieked.

He laughed again. "OK. Probably have on a robe and cream all over your face, right?"

She startled that he could be so perceptive, at least about the robe. "Well, I'm not—"

"Actually, I'm surprised to find you there."

"I—had letters to write, and—"

He interrupted. "Have you had dinner?"

A rumbling in her stomach made her remember that she hadn't. "Uh, no, but—"

"Do you like seafood?"

"Well, yes—"

"So do I. Throw some clothes on. Nothing fancy.

Jeans are OK. I'll meet you in the bar in fifteen minutes.''

"Fifteen minutes? But you don't understand. First of all, I don't drink and secondly, you simply must—'' But she was talking to a dial tone.

Piqued that he would be so presumptuous, she took him at his word and dressed in a pair of jeans and a pink sweater. As a somewhat defiant gesture, perhaps to prove a point to Aaron Steele that she wasn't about to conform to the ways of Hollywood, she pulled on her comfortable and well-worn western boots and grabbed her favorite buckskin jacket.

She'd straighten him out right away. Meet him in the bar, indeed! He probably was on his second or third drink by now. Maybe he had no intention of going to dinner. Maybe he thought she would stay right there with him and drink. Well, Mr. Aaron Steele had another think coming!

By the time she reached the bar and went inside, she was filled with indignation and annoyance and strained her eyes to find him in the dimly-lit room. He was in a corner booth, motioning her to join him.

She marched to the booth and sat down. When the cocktail waitress asked her what she wanted, she primly replied, "Nothing." Before he could speak, she started right in.

"You may as well know, first of all," she said, "that I think it was rude of you to hang up on me. Secondly, I don't drink and I resent meeting someone in a bar. Thirdly, if you're just going to sit here and get drunk, we may as well say good night right here and now!''

A dark eyebrow winged upward. "Are you finished?'' he asked quietly.

She flushed. "Yes."

He took a sip from his glass. Then he leaned toward her until his face was only inches from her own. Bethany was held transfixed.

"First of all, sweetheart, I'll agree with you. It was rude of me to hang up like that. I just didn't want an argument because I need to talk to you. Secondly, the reason I asked you to meet me in the bar is because this room is rather dark, you may have noticed, and I am not as conspicuous. Had I waited for you in the lobby, you would have found me surrounded by autograph seekers. Thirdly, I am pleased that you don't drink because neither do I. This is a soft drink I am having." He moved even closer, until she felt his warm breath on her face. "Now then, I am starved. If you want to have dinner with me, fine. If you don't I'll go by myself." His eyes lowered to her mouth and she couldn't even swallow. "Well?" he persisted.

She nodded. "All right." She felt humiliated and ashamed. What a terrible way to start a relationship! And after Cal had warned her to be careful of her attitude!

When they were in the well-lighted lobby, he took in her attire with an amused smile. "Is it outside?" he asked.

She looked up at him in puzzlement. "Is what outside?"

"Your horse," he replied. "Surely you brought your horse with you?"

Bethany's face turned beet red but she said nothing. How dare he make fun of her!

Sensing her discomfort, he took her arm. The physical contact caused gooseflesh to appear, and she was grateful for the jacket she had on. "I'm sorry," he said softly. "I wasn't making fun of you, Beth. In fact, I like your outfit."

She lowered her head. *Will I ever get used to this man?* she thought. "Thank you," she said.

The restaurant was in Santa Monica. It was not an elegant place but more of a family-type restaurant and the food was delicious. Their table was next to a window where they could look out at the sea.

He helped her off with her jacket, and they sat down and as he studied the menu, she studied him, admiring the way he looked. He also wore jeans, and a fisherman's sweater. The sweater was white and a stark but flattering contrast to his dark brown hair and eyes, so thickly fringed with black lashes.

When the waitress served their salad, Bethany dragged her eyes from his handsome face. She knew she had to apologize.

"I'm sorry for the way I acted back there," she said. "I had no right to sound so defensive."

"No problem," he said with a grin. "We're all entitled to blow off a little steam now and then."

"Yes, but it wasn't fair of me, to just presume things. And I'm certain my attitude didn't please God."

He looked at her thoughtfully. "Do you always think about that?"

"What?"

"Pleasing God?"

"Well, I try to. Yes."

He looked down at his salad and took a large bite before speaking again. "What about the changes I requested in the script? How do you feel about them?"

"I have mixed feelings."

"Such as?"

"Well, I can see your point about Salome. It may be confusing to some who aren't that familiar with people mentioned in the Bible. We can work around that, I'm sure. I don't think that will be a problem."

He smiled. "What about the rest?"

"Well, I don't think you should feel uncomfortable about leaning against Jesus' breast at the scene of the Last Supper. That's very Scriptural."

"I realize that it is. Maybe it's that I can't stand the actor they've signed up to play Jesus."

"Why should that matter? Can't you put those feelings aside? You *are* an actor, Aaron, a very fine actor."

He looked at her in astonishment. "You don't have to tell me that, sweetheart!" he said hotly.

She was grateful for the momentary interruption when the waitress brought their seafood plate, a delicious assortment of white fish, shrimp, and scallops. The last thing she wanted to do was offend this man. "Please God," she prayed silently, "give me the right words. Instill in me some of Your gentleness."

"What I meant to say," he said, looking at him, "is that actors have the ability to regard only the character that is being portrayed, don't they?"

He nodded and studied the plate of seafood. "Yes. But you don't know this guy. He's a real—"

"Can't you think only of the part he's playing?" she interrupted. "Can't you just focus on Jesus?"

He looked at her shrewdly. "I'm sure it would be easier for someone like you, who's so buddy-buddy with God!"

She spread her hands in frustration. "Oh, please! I

didn't mean to offend you!" She didn't know what to say next.

He sulked a moment, then shrugged. "I'll give it a good try."

She smiled. "Oh, good! That's half the battle!"

"What about the other objection I had, about—"

She interrupted. "Don't you think we could continue another time with that one?" She knew his objection to John's character change was something that would necessitate a lengthy discussion. And she felt that it should be preceded by some evidence—some proof from the Scriptures that it did happen. But she sensed that Aaron Steele wasn't in a receptive enough mood for that right now.

He stared at her a moment, his dark eyes deep and unfathomable. "I apologize, Beth," he said. "No dinner conversation should be all business."

"I didn't mean—I just think that we should take one potato at a time."

He laughed. "You're a cute girl, do you know that?"

Her cheeks flushed pink. "I–I never thought of myself as cute," she said awkwardly. "And I'm not a girl, in case you haven't noticed!" she said, suddenly hating herself for sounding so rebellious.

His eyes narrowed. "Oh, I have noticed! You seem to be all woman, but I haven't had the opportunity yet to find out." Before she could think of an appropriate answer, he went on with a sly grin. "You can't be more than about twenty-five. And since I'm thirty-one, anyone still in her twenties is a girl to me."

She pushed her now empty plate to one side. "I am twenty-five, exactly. And thirty-one isn't old, you know."

"I'm glad you feel that way." He paused and looked at her in the same way he had looked at so many actresses on the screen. A long, sexy look. A look that said, "I want you." Bethany inadvertently trembled. "Do you want dessert?" he asked in a half-whisper.

His tone startled her, and a reckless thought went zipping through her mind. *What if he tries to kiss me?*

She fought desperately to push the thought aside. Avoiding his eyes she replied in a halting voice, "Uh—no, thank you. Not tonight!"

The feelings Bethany experienced that night when she returned to her hotel room were confusing. Aaron Steele had stirred up something inside her that no man had done before. Though the only physical contact they had was when he touched her arm, he had made her feel passion—the desperate need for restraint. And it wasn't because he was a famous and romantic actor. Had he been an accountant it would be the same. The fact remained that Aaron Steele was a man—all man. Well over six feet of desirable male that she suddenly longed for. She found herself wishing she could know the strength of his arms around her; hear his whispered words of passion; feel the thrill of his lips on hers.

She dropped to her knees, tears brimming in her eyes. "Oh, God! Heavenly Father! Why is this happening to me? Help me control it, for these feelings are new to me! Dear Lord, please—I pray that I may not have the opportunity to have to decide what to do. But if the temptations do come, help me resist this man!"

CHAPTER 3

BETHANY DID NOT SEE or hear from Aaron Steele the next morning. Perhaps the Lord arranged this, she thought. Maybe He was blessing her with not having to fight temptation.

Several times during the morning she thought about Aaron and the dinner they enjoyed at the little seafood restaurant and the need the actor had to discuss with her his requested changes in the script. He had softened on one or two things, yet he had been adamant in his stand that John's character should not be different toward the end of the play.

She prayed for an open door—something that would prove to Aaron Steele that the character change in John really took place, and would happen to anyone that accepted Jesus. If Aaron could just see proof of this, it would better enable him to understand the part and play it the way she wanted it done. No, correction. The way *God* wanted it done. Aaron Steele, she mused, was much like John in the beginning—before John experienced the life changing blessings of Jesus Christ. Both men were quite opinionated and anything but humble.

"Please, God," she prayed aloud. "Help Aaron see the truth. Help him know You, for You *are* the truth."

She thought of the drive home from the restaurant the night before and how quiet the actor had been. When he dropped her off at the hotel, she thanked him for dinner, and he said, "We'll do it again. See you later!"

But Bethany didn't know what he meant by "later." It could be later in the week, later in the month. . . .

Much as she hated to admit it, she had actually been disappointed that he had not tried to even hold her hand. And yet, she thought ashamedly, why would Aaron Steele show any romantic interest in Bethany Jordan? He saw her last night because she wrote the play he was going to be in and he needed to discuss the script. Nothing more. He would undoubtedly see her many more times for the same reason. But never for anything else.

Maybe God would turn it into a blessing, though. Maybe through these discussions, the Lord would use her as an instrument in bringing Aaron Steele to Jesus! She smiled at the hopeful thought.

She sighed and opened her closet to select something appropriate for the meeting that afternoon. Lifting the teal-blue suit out of the closet, she frowned at it and hung it back up again. It was a nice suit and she wanted to look appropriate. Professional. But . . .

"Help me decide, Lord," she asked.

She remembered one of her girl friends in her

church back home that criticized her for asking God's assistance in "trivial" things like that. But Bethany was a firm believer that the Lord cared about every facet of her life, big or small, including the right outfit for an important meeting like the one scheduled this afternoon.

And it was important. Cal had informed her on the phone that this was one of several meetings that would take place in which the breakdown of the script would be done. The TV script editors were craftsmen too, Cal explained, and would work with her. From the breakdown, they would go on to the finished script.

It was all new to Bethany. She thought she had finished the script. She was not aware all these steps had to take place, even though she thought she had learned all there was to learn when doing research at the public library back home.

Another surprise was when Cal told her the scenes would be shot in fragments and not necessarily in order of the play. Yet she was expected to keep and achieve a sense of continuity in the script. Cal had told her though, that she was the only one privileged to regard the play as an entity. The director, and others, such as the set designers, would break the script up into segments, and after all the pieces were filmed, it would be put back together again by the film editors.

Bethany shook her head in confusion. She hoped the editors would be more successful than all the king's men who tried to reassemble Humpty Dumpty.

At any rate, she might be more enlightened after today's meeting. A lot of those details would come up this afternoon, and she did want to conduct herself properly and feel confident.

And—she had to look right as well. God knew that, too. Automatically, she reached in her closet and removed a shrimp-colored shirtwaist dress and put it on.

"That's perfect!" she said out loud as she looked in the mirror. "Thank you, Lord!"

She smiled to herself as she thought of all the conversations she had carried on with God. How caring he was about her—about all His own. And how caring and patient He was about those that did not yet belong to Him.

The phone interrupted her ruminations. It was Calvin Bruce.

"Hi, Bethany! Everything OK?"

"Fine, thanks!"

"Ready for this afternoon's session?"

"I feel a little like I'm about to be fed to lions, but yes—I'm ready!"

He chuckled. "Meeting's at two o'clock. I'll pick you up about one-thirty, OK?"

"OK, Cal. I'll be ready."

"Don't forget to keep an open mind."

"I'll remember!"

When she hung up the phone she wondered if Aaron Steele would be there.

There were several script editors at the meeting. One was a woman by the name of Sheila Cross who had a smile that didn't seem genuine. Another was a man that Bethany felt an affinity for right away, for some reason. His name was Franklin McKenzie.

Mike Innes, the producer, was not there, and for a moment Bethany thought that meant that Aaron Steele would not show up either, but she was wrong.

He walked in just as they were about to discuss the title of the play.

The actor gave Bethany a totally captivating smile and winked before he sat down, the effects of which caused goose bumps on her arms. She was grateful the dress she wore had long sleeves.

"I've discussed the title with Mike," Sheila Cross began. "Mike doesn't think much of it and neither do I. I don't think anyone will know what 'agape' means."

Cal glanced at Bethany with a concerned expression to see her reaction to the blunt statement, but she remained calm, inwardly praying that God would have His way, if He thought the title was right.

The man called Franklin McKenzie spoke up. "I disagree, Sheila," he said. "The word 'agape' is one of the Greek words used for love in the New Testament, but it's unlike any other word, really. 'Agape' is loving and forgiving someone even when they don't deserve it. It's the kind of love God has for us." He smiled at Bethany.

Her heart leaped in response. *He talks like a Christian!* she thought hopefully. She smiled back.

"I think we should let the title stay as it is," Franklin continued. "We can explain it through dialogue, for the benefit of those that don't know the meaning of the word. But frankly, Sheila, I think a lot of more people than you realize, know what it means. Anyway, I like it."

Sheila narrowed her eyes and remained silent. A discussion followed, pro and con, but Bethany could see that Franklin was winning out. The convincing argument in favor of the title, surprisingly, came from Aaron.

"I have to agree with Franklin," he said. "I'll admit I wasn't sure about it at first but the idea of clarifying the meaning through dialogue appeals to me. And it has a good sound to it." He looked at the ceiling. "'Agape, John,'" he said thoughtfully. "Yes, I like it." He looked at Bethany and grinned broadly as if to tell her one point had just been settled.

And it was. The title stood as she had written it. She made notes to do some rewrite on dialogue concerning this, and she noted Cal was making notes, too.

"On the matter of John leaning against the bosom of Jesus," Sheila said, "I think we can cut that out, Aaron, if you're uncomfortable with it."

Bethany could feel her patience ebbing. "But it's scriptural!" she blurted out. Cal shot her a warning look and she reddened.

Much to her amazement, Aaron spoke up in her favor. "Beth is right," he said. "It is scriptural. I don't like that no-good drunk they've hired to play Jesus, but—"

Calvin interrupted. "Glenn Davidson? I heard he's on the wagon, Aaron. Hasn't had a drink in months."

Aaron grunted unbelievingly. "Huh! I'll believe that when I see it!"

Franklin turned to the actor. "Glenn Davidson doesn't drink anymore, Aaron. He's been converted."

"He's been what?"

Franklin's reply was quiet, gentle. "He's accepted Christ."

Sheila rolled her eyes to the ceiling as if to say, "Oh, no! Not another one of those!"

Calvin caught the woman's expression and frowned

at her, then gave his attention to the actor again. "So what's the bottom line, Aaron? Does the scene stay in or not?"

"It stays," he said. "I promised Beth I'd give it a try, even though I don't have any use for Glenn Davidson, converted or not!"

Calvin glanced at Bethany and raised his eyebrows. There were questions in his eyes as to when, where, and how Aaron Steele had made that promise. "You work fast, Aaron," he said with a touch of sarcasm.

"Not as fast as I'd like to," the actor replied, giving Bethany another of those looks that turned her legs into jelly.

The rest of the meeting covered a multitude of things. She was informed that they were working with a tight budget and had to limit exteriors to one or two. The rest of the exteriors would have to be implied through dialogue. More rewrite.

She learned a lot of new terminology. Though, by the time she had finished writing her play, she had become familiar with such technical terms as "fade in" and "fade out," much as she would have used the rising and falling of a curtain on a stage, there were other words and phrases used at the meeting by the professionals in attendance, that were unfamiliar to her. "Dolly in," she found, was used when the camera moved in on an object or person to give the viewers a better look. She had used the term, "move in," which was technically correct. But since the camera was mounted on a low frame on wheels, which made it very mobile, "dolly in" and "dolly back," which meant the opposite, seemed to be the preferred terminology.

And so it went for the remainder of the meeting, with Bethany's mind soaking up bits of information like a sponge and her fingers cramping from taking so many notes.

Aaron rose to leave and winked at Bethany before slipping out the door. The wink was, unfortunately, witnessed by Sheila Cross, who smiled sweetly at Aaron but looked at Bethany with venom.

Bethany concluded that most women who ever gazed on the handsome face of Aaron Steele, probably fell madly in love with him and that Sheila was no exception. That he had openly admitted a more private meeting with Bethany, no doubt triggered a response of jealousy from Sheila Cross, unfounded as it was.

After the meeting, Bethany and Calvin were in the parking lot, heading toward his car, when Franklin McKenzie called out. "Cal, can I talk to you a minute?"

"Sure." He opened the door to the car and Bethany climbed in. "I'll just be a minute," he said to her.

The two men were a distance away and Bethany couldn't hear what they were saying. They talked for quite a few minutes, and she saw Cal shrug, then nod his head in agreement a few times. Then Franklin smiled and waved to her and she waved back as she watched him walk to his own car.

Cal got in and started the ignition. "Franklin's got a good idea," he said. "But it's all up to you."

"What's that?"

"Well, he asked me where you were staying and I told him. He's concerned about you living at a hotel."

"It's a nice hotel."

"I know. But he was considering the expense for one thing, and there's no one around for you to talk to, you know."

"That's very thoughtful of him, but—"

"You may as well face it, honey," he said. "You'll be here for some time. You could always stay at my place, but I don't suppose you'd go for that." He shot her a questioning look.

"No. Thank you, but I couldn't do that."

"No. Of course not." He sighed and lit a cigarette, inhaling deeply. "Well anyway, Franklin and his wife Nora, have a really nice house in the Valley, and there's plenty of room. Nora's younger sister was staying with them but she's away at college, and Franklin said you'd be welcome to stay with them and use that spare room. He's a decent sort, Bethany. Happily married and all. They have a cute little boy too, named Timothy. And they're like you, you know."

"Like me?"

"Yeah, you know—they're Christians." He said it as if he were describing a particular race, and Bethany had to smile.

"That's very nice. I thought he was a Christian the way he talked at the meeting today," she said happily. "And I'll certainly give it some thought. I wouldn't want to impose on them, though."

"He wouldn't have suggested it, if he thought you would be. What do you say?"

"I'll pray about it."

"Oh. OK."

Cal took her to dinner that night at a restaurant on LaCienega Boulevard.

"I'd like to see you go on with this idea," he said.

"What idea?"

"Writing other TV plays about Bible characters. Maybe not as long as 'Agape, John.' Probably more like half hour or one hour scripts. You know, single out a different character each week from the Bible. Think you could do it?"

"Are you talking about a series?"

"Something like that. We'll have to see how this one does in the ratings first, but my guess is that it will score pretty high."

"Really? How can you be so sure?"

"I can't. Just a gut feeling. The scene is always changing. Always. Each new season brings another surprise. As I say, it's just a feeling that I have. Besides, you've certainly created a good work in 'Agape, John.' Though most people know that the characters told about in the Bible were once real people, there is still, sometimes, a kind of fairy-tale quality about them. But you've given them flesh and blood and three dimensions. You've woven your play around real situations and problems and your characters are individualized. That's good. Anyway, aside from all that, I just think the public is ready for something like your play."

"I hope so. I really hope so. I've prayed hard about it."

"I'm sure you have." He took a bite of steak, and a pensive look crossed his face. "I like you, Beth."

"I like you too, Cal. You've become a good friend to me in the short time we've known each other."

"I don't want to see you hurt. You can, you know."

"How could I get hurt?"

"You're vulnerable."

"How's that?"

"Aaron Steele. Don't let him hurt you, honey."

The food seemed to form a large lump and stick half way down to her stomach. "What—what do you mean?"

"He uses women, honey. Like facial tissues, if you get my point."

She gave him a level look. "Well, this is one woman Mr. Aaron Steele is not going to use and throw away! Don't you worry, Cal. I may not be from Hollywood, but I have a little more than sagebrush between my ears! I do know what is going on! Now, don't worry, OK?" She gave a light laugh and wished she felt as convincing as she sounded.

Bethany had no sooner entered her hotel room when the phone rang. Her heart leaped treacherously when she answered it and heard the deep, familiar voice on the other end of the line. He must have been waiting for her to get home, she thought, and she didn't know just how to react to that.

"I thought you'd never get home! Where did he take you?"

"Oh! Aaron! Uh—a restaurant on La—something."

"LaCienega."

"Yes, that's it."

"Restaurant Row, it's been called. That was nice of him. Cal's OK. I like him."

"I'm glad you approve!"

"As your agent, I mean!"

"Yes—well, that's what he is. And my friend." Cal's warnings shot through her mind.

"I'd like to see you."

"When?"

"Now. Can I come up?"

"No!"

"Well, I can't take you to dinner because you've already eaten. I certainly can't take you for cocktails since neither of us indulge. And if you won't let me come up to your room, then I surely can't take you to my place, can I? How about a drive along the coast?"

"Oh! I think I'd like that! Only it is getting late and Cal said there was another meeting tomorrow, and it's scheduled pretty early in the morning, so—"

"No more excuses. Come on down. I'll be in the bar with my usual soft drink."

The drive was beautiful, even if it was a little too chilly to roll down the window. He took a turn suddenly, off the main highway and onto a narrow road, until they were parked facing the ocean, where he switched off the ignition.

Bethany's pulse quickened at the intimacy of the moment.

He leaned back. "Tell me more about yourself, Beth."

His inquiry was unexpected and caught her off-guard. "Me?"

"Yes. Why are you so surprised?"

"Oh, I–I don't know. Except that there's not much to tell."

"I'll decide that. I promise, if I get bored, you'll be the first to know!"

She laughed lightly. "OK, that's a deal!" She began to relax a little. "Well, I've been writing all my life. I had several plays done by little theater groups. I just kept writing in the early hours of the morning and working during the day."

"And at night?"

She flushed a little. "Research. At the library."

"Oh. What kind of work did you do during the day?"

"I waited tables."

"Honest? Why that?"

"I liked it, for one thing. But mostly, I didn't have to use my mind much, so my brain didn't get all burned out as it may have with another kind of job."

"That makes sense. And your family?"

"Parents living and well, back home. I have a younger brother in school."

"What do your parents do?"

"My dad owns a hardware store in town and Mom helps him."

"I thought maybe you lived on a ranch or something."

She laughed. "Not everyone in Colorado lives on a ranch. We're fairly close to Denver and that's a pretty big city!"

"Oh, I know that. But you're not in Denver, you said, and I just assumed. . . ."

"There are ranches and farms all around us," she said. "We live in a pretty rural area."

"I see. No boyfriends? Lovers?"

"No." She changed the subject quickly. "What about you? How did you become an actor?"

For an instant she felt somewhat strange, asking Aaron Steele such a question. But the instant passed, and it seemed comfortable to talk to him about his private life.

"I've always wanted to act, ever since I was a kid.

Just like you and your writing. For a while I worked in a bank because my father's a banker, but I hated it. I don't think my parents were ever too happy about my acting career. Except now, of course, because I'm finally established."

"Are your parents living here?"

"Right here in Los Angeles! Dad's still at the bank. I don't think he'll ever retire. And Mom busies herself with women's clubs and church activities. I don't have any brothers or sisters."

"Church activities?"

"Oh, yes. I was raised to go to church every Sunday whether I wanted to or not! You'd never know it now, would you?"

"I think it's rather evident at times!"

He reached across the back of the seat and wound a strand of her hair around his finger. Her heart pounded.

"Look at us," he said huskily. "I actually brought you out to discuss the play, and we haven't done a bit of it yet!"

"Th—there's time for that," she whispered, not realizing how seductive she sounded.

"I'd rather be doing other things right now," he said softly.

"Yes—uh—well, it is late, Aaron. Maybe we'd— uh—better . . ."

He stopped playing with her hair. "You're really up tight, aren't you?"

"I just think we should be—careful, that's all."

"Careful?"

"Not to get too carried away."

He gave an exasperated sigh. "You're sure not liberated, are you?"

39

She struggled to keep her voice steady. "On the contrary," she said gently. "I was liberated the moment I accepted Jesus into my heart."

He looked at her enigmatically. "How long are you going to stick to that part?"

"Part? Being a Christian isn't a part! It's a total commitment!"

"Don't Christians even believe in one kiss?"

Her heart suddenly thundered, matching the pounding of the waves on the shore. She ran moist palms together nervously. "I—of course, Aaron. It's just a question of knowing when to—to stop."

He reached for her then, and Bethany was amazed at the gentleness with which he drew her close to him. Cupping her chin, he raised her face to meet his. Then he kissed her.

Bethany tried to convince herself that the reason her head was spinning was because she was being kissed by the handsome actor, Aaron Steele, but that simply was not true. Though it was certainly evident that he was master of the art of love-making, Bethany knew there was something else. Something different about the way the blood was rushing through her veins and pounding in her head as his mouth took full possession of hers. The kiss went on and on, deepening in passion and intensity until she wanted to cry out, Help me Lord! I'm getting into a dangerous area!

Some inner force gave her the strength to slowly push away from him. Her throat was dry when she spoke in a barely audible whisper. "I—think we'd better go, Aaron."

His hands moved from her back to her slender shoulders where they tightened their hold on her. He stared at her for a moment, with an expression that was unfathomable, and said nothing. He just continued to look at her silently in the half light, his fingers digging into her soft flesh. Then he released his grip on her and his hands slid down her arms. His fingers seemed to ignite everywhere they touched.

Aaron remained strangely silent all the way back, driving with a set jaw and eyes not leaving the road.

Please God, she silently prayed. *Help him understand.*

An overpowering longing surged within her, and she prayed that God would hold back her tears, because she knew a deluge was certainly coming. Tears of passion—of longing—of regret? No, not regret.

Bethany knew she had a long night of prayer ahead of her.

CHAPTER 4

DESPITE THE LACK OF sleep Bethany had the night before, she awoke early Friday morning feeling refreshed. She had spent a considerable amount of time in prayer before going to sleep and knew God was responsible for her rested condition. She even had some time to do a little work on the script before Cal picked her up.

The meeting was difficult and long. Perhaps it was because Aaron never showed up, although she really didn't expect that he would. Through the first part of the meeting her thoughts wandered to him wondering if one of the reasons for his absence was because of the night before and her unwillingness to continue with his amorous advances. Maybe he had no patience with her "kind." For a few brief moments she tortured herself with images of Aaron spending time that morning with some very willing, very sexy actress.

Then she abruptly forced her attention away from

Aaron Steele and back to the meeting. For one thing, it was important for her to concentrate on what was going on here and now, she told herself. And in the second place, God did not want her to dwell on any situation that even bordered on jealousy and that's just what it was, she thought gloomily. She was beginning to have strong feelings for Aaron Steele and was somewhat resentful of the fact that there were women out there who would gladly continue where she left off.

She remembered reading in the Song of Solomon that "jealousy was as cruel as the grave." That was quite probably true, she thought, since jealousy certainly had the power to put an end to a relationship.

Once her mother confessed that when she was first married, she was jealous of a young, pretty girl that worked at the hardware store. Without discussing it with Bethany's father or even asking the Lord to intervene, the jealousy grew into an absolute monster. Every time she looked at the young girl working near her husband, she imagined she saw something between them that simply was not true.

"It's strange how the mind will work," she told Bethany. "I was almost ready to leave your father when I decided, finally, to pray about it. Something I should have done months before. The next day a young man came to the store to pick up the girl and introduced himself as her fiancé. I realized how foolish I had been. I told your father then, and asked his forgiveness."

Her mother had lectured Bethany quite strongly about three important things. The most vital, she said, was in taking every problem to the Lord immediately, which was what God wanted His children to do. The second was to not let a seed of jealousy begin to grow, and the third, was to remember the importance of keeping a line of communication open between husband and wife, or in any relationship.

Bethany considered her mother's words. Certain feelings were taking root in her and she had to do something about them right away.

"Help me, Lord," she prayed silently. "Help me concentrate on this meeting and not on Aaron Steele, and especially help me to fight any feelings of jealousy and resentment. And lust," she added, a little hesitantly. "Because I know those feelings do not belong in me."

The rest of the meeting went fairly smoothly.

Cal wasted no time helping her move from the hotel to the home of Franklin and Nora McKenzie.

He carried her suitcases to the car and even whistled as he drove her to her new living quarters.

The McKenzie's home was in a nice, quiet neighborhood, with a park and playground only a block away.

Frank was already home and though he seemed to be a little surprised that she was there so soon, he was nonetheless, pleased to see her and introduced her to his wife, Nora.

"I'm so happy you can stay with us, Bethany," Nora said. "The spare room is just sitting idle and there's no sense in that!"

"Well, I'm really grateful that you asked me. It's a comfortable hotel, but—"

"But after awhile, any hotel gets pretty tiring!" Nora interrupted. "Have you had dinner?"

"Uh, no."

"Good! Come on! We're just getting ready to eat. How about you, Cal? Can you stay for dinner?"

"No, thanks, Nora. I'm going out. But I'll take a raincheck."

"You're on!"

So by six o'clock that evening, Bethany was moved, bag and baggage, and the grin on Calvin's face as he left was somewhat amusing. It seemed to tell her that he now considered her to be in a "safe place."

Safe from Aaron Steele, probably!

Bethany liked Calvin Bruce. He was a kind man, a considerate man. He was quite obviously attracted to her but that didn't look like it would be a problem. In spite of the attraction—or perhaps because of it—he had appointed himself as her protector and guardian.

She prayed for God to give her an open door to witness to Calvin. He was not a Christian but certainly showed respect for her beliefs. And he seemed quite friendly with the McKenzies who, she found out immediately, were really on fire for the Lord.

As they sat around the McKenzie dinner table, she praised God for giving her this Christian fellowship while she was away from home.

Their son Timothy, an adorable little boy of six, insisted on sitting next to Bethany at the table and asked if he could say a blessing.

"Thank you God, for our food. And we sure do appreciate that you sent this nice lady to stay with us. Amen."

Bethany's eyes misted. "Thank you, Timothy. I appreciate that!"

He grinned and Nora had to remind him that his dinner was in front of him.

As soon as they finished eating, Timothy ran to his room and came back with an assortment of prized toy cars to show her.

"This one's a '57 Chevy," he explained proudly, "and this is a Model A Ford, and this—"

"Timothy," Nora began gently, "don't you think it would be a good idea if we let Bethany unpack her things first?"

"Oh, sure!" he said excitedly. "Can I help?"

Bethany ruffled the soft blonde curls on his head. "I don't see why not," she said with a smile. "But first I'll help your mom with the dishes, OK?"

"Frank bought me a dishwasher last month so there's no need for that," Nora replied. "But you can help clear the table if you want. Timmy, you too."

"Aw, Mom—"

"Timothy?"

"OK." Though his smile faded, he began to obediently pick up the silverware.

Nora covered the leftover pieces of chicken with plastic wrap and put the platter in the fridge, while Bethany looked around the modest kitchen in admiration.

It was typically "Americana," with stenciled cupboard doors, herbs hung from hooks, drying in the window over the sink, and homey, colorful rag runners on the floor. Near the stove was an oversize antique crock that housed kitchen utensils and adorning the walls were various plaques with Christian messages on them.

It was comfortable and reminded her a little of the family kitchen back home. It reflected the love of a family unit, somehow. She couldn't help but wonder how it compared with a kitchen of a single man, such as Aaron or Calvin Bruce.

Tearing off a sheet of the plastic wrap she placed it over the bowl of peas, smoothing the wrap down over the sides of the bowl thoughtfully. "What about Cal?" she asked.

"What about Cal?"

"Do you know him pretty well?"

"Pretty well. He's here a lot. He's a really nice person."

"Yes, he is," Bethany agreed. "He isn't saved," she added reflectively.

"No, but we're working on that!"

"You are? You and Franklin?"

"And all our friends," Nora said with a smile. "Cal seems almost fascinated by our lifestyle. I mean, let's face it, it's quite different from his own. We've invited him to our Bible study groups, and he came to one of them, but he seemed uncomfortable and left early."

"Maybe he's under conviction."

"Maybe. But he'll come around sooner or later, so many of us are praying for him!"

"That's wonderful! Do you have Bible studies here often?"

"About once a week, but they're not always here. We rotate homes. Tuesday is the next one though, and it will be here. If you have anyone you'd care to invite . . ."

She thought of Aaron. "Well, now that you mention it . . ."

The doorbell interrupted them and they heard Franklin answer it. Nora strained to hear who it was, then shrugged. "No voice I recognize," she said. "Probably a friend of Frank's."

But Bethany knew the familiar deep voice, and the bowl of peas froze in her hands. As he came into the kitchen, she said, "Aaron! What a surprise!"

Nora nervously smoothed her hair. "Oh, uh—gee! Aaron Steele! Wow! In my kitchen!"

He laughed. "You must be Nora," he said, extending his hand. "I'm very happy to know you."

Nora's face flushed as she continued to stare at the handsome actor, until Franklin cleared his throat.

"Aaron came to see Bethany about the script, Nora."

"Oh, yes! Well! Shall I make coffee?"

"Not for me, thank you," he replied with a smile. Turning to Bethany, his smile disappeared. "I had a time finding you, Beth," he said. "When I learned you had checked out of the hotel I tried to reach Cal because I figured he would know where you were, but he wasn't home. I called fourteen restaurants before I found him." He stood close to her now, looking down at her with annoyance.

"It all happened pretty fast!" she said, keeping her voice as light as possible.

"I wondered if we could take a drive? Talk over the script?"

"Well—uh—yes. Sure!"

"Is now an appropriate time? I can't stay out too late. I have an early call in the morning."

"Now," she repeated, trancelike. "Oh, yes! Now! Sure, fine with me!" She chuckled nervously and noticed a sagacious grin on Nora's face.

"Is that coming along, too?"

"That?"

"That. The bowl of peas you're hanging on to."

"Peas? Oh, for heaven's sake! No, of course not! I'll just put it in the fridge!"

Nora was still giggling when they left.

He drove to the same spot by the sea, and Bethany was as close to the door as possible, curls of apprehension forming in her stomach.

"I saw Glenn today," he said.

"Glenn?"

"Glenn Davidson, the lush."

"Oh, yes. You mean the ex-lush, don't you?"

"I don't know that yet. Although he was sober today, for a change. He's not a bad sort, when he's sober."

"I'm sure he's not," she said gently. She silently offered a prayer of thanks for the conversion of Glenn Davidson. "You think you'll be able to work with him OK?"

"I made you a promise, didn't I? I never go back on my word, Beth."

"Thank you. That's an admirable trait."

He changed the subject. "Frank's an all right person. You'll like staying with the McKenzies."

"I know. It was nice of Cal to arrange it for me, wasn't it?"

"Oh, yes. Cal. I forgot for a minute that he hauled you over there. Surprised you aren't out with him tonight."

"Aaron, Cal and I are just friends. Besides, I shouldn't think it would matter to you that much. Ours is still pretty much a business relationship, isn't it?"

He looked at her intently. "Is it?"

Bethany looked down at her interlacing hands and tried to keep her voice steady. "You said you wanted to discuss the script, Aaron."

He sighed. "Yes, I do. But you needn't glue yourself to the door like it's an escape hatch, Beth. I won't bite you."

She edged toward him an inch or two, feeling childish and immature and wondering if that was how he thought of her.

For the next hour they talked about nothing but the script, but strangely enough, he never brought up the subject of the character change in John, which Bethany thought would be the first thing he would want to discuss.

Then he looked at the luminous dial of his watch. "I'd better take you back now, I guess. I have to get up at four."

"Four? Heavens! Why so early?"

"Some commercial I got talked into, and wish I hadn't. Anyway, I'm to be an Arab sheik, and we're going out into the desert on location to shoot. I don't know how Vivian will ever get up that early," he added with a chuckle.

"Vivian?"

"Vivian Gordon. Every sheik has to have at least one beautiful woman by his side," he said playfully.

Bethany knew full well who Vivian Gordon was. Probably the most voluptuous actress to appear on the screen in some time. The flawless features of the brunette could be seen gracing at least one or two magazine covers every month, sultry dark eyes gazing seductively at the camera, beneath their thick, mascara-coated lashes.

He started the ignition. "Vivian and I are just friends," he said. "Like you and Cal." There was sarcasm in his voice.

Bethany said nothing.

They drove along in silence for a while before he spoke again. "Look, I have no idea when we'll get back tomorrow, but it shouldn't be too late. How about a no-business dinner?"

She laughed. "I'd like that!"

"And we can go dancing if you like. To a respectable place, I promise."

"OK," she said with a smile.

"I'll call you when I get back."

"How long should I wait for your call?"

"Six-thirty. If I don't call by then, go ahead and eat."

"All right."

When he pulled up in front of the house he reached for her hand and squeezed it. "I won't come in, Beth. I really need to go home and get some sleep."

"I understand that, Aaron. Good night, and good luck tomorrow."

"Thanks. Good night, Beth."

For most of Saturday, Bethany worked on the rewrite and listened to the pouring rain outside. Periodically, her thoughts wandered to Aaron, wondering if they really went on location in this inclement weather. Or perhaps it wasn't raining in the desert? She had no idea, but half expected him to call during the day to tell her the trip had been cancelled. Every time the phone rang she jumped and Nora and Frank teased her a little about being "anxious."

She thought of Vivian Gordon and the actress' shaky reputation. Though Bethany had not seen the R-rated movies, she had heard that Vivian had appeared nude in several films. Again, she wondered just how friendly Vivian was with Aaron. The actor's morals seemed to be on a much higher level though. And she had no recollection of reading about Aaron Steele appearing sans clothing in any motion picture. Of course, that was no criteria by which she could form an opinion, since his roles were primarily done for television.

By six o'clock it was still pouring rain and Bethany was convinced he would call her any moment, so she bathed and dressed in a periwinkle blue jersey dress that had a modest neckline, but clung rather tightly over the bust.

"Is this too revealing?" she asked Nora.

Nora studied the dress a moment. "No, I don't think so. You're certainly well covered. The neckline is pretty high and the sleeves are three-quarter—"

"Actually, I was thinking of the way it clings to my figure."

"Well, you are well-blessed in certain places," Nora said with a twinkle in her eyes. "I shouldn't think you'd be able to hide it, though, no matter what you wore."

Bethany flushed. "I know—well, I just wanted to make sure the dress is all right."

"Beth, are you certain he'll call? It's almost six-thirty now."

"Oh, yes! I mean, look at the weather. How can they shoot in that?"

Nora smiled. "The desert is probably dry," she said patiently. "Dinner's all ready. Don't you want to eat?"

"No, I'll wait for his call, thanks. It shouldn't be much longer!"

Nora shrugged. "OK. But if you get hungry—"

"If I get hungry, I can find my way to the kitchen," she said, laughing. "I'll just go ahead with my work while I'm waiting. I really have a lot to do."

For a while Bethany became totally caught up in her work and it wasn't until Nora knocked at the open doorway at her room that she looked up.

"It's eight o'clock, Bethany. Don't you want to eat something now?"

"Eight o'clock?" she gasped. "I had no idea. I guess he must have been detained. I suppose I will just have a sandwich or something."

With a touch of disappointment, Bethany fixed a cold cheese sandwich and some potato salad leftover from lunch. She had no sooner finished it when the phone rang.

"It's for you," Nora said with a wink. Then she whispered, "I think it's him!"

Bethany ran to the phone. "Hello?"

"Hi there! I'm really sorry I got back so late. Did you have dinner yet?"

"Yes. Well, you said—"

"I know what I said. Look, I'll grab a snack and shower and change clothes. I'll pick you up in about forty-five minutes."

Aaron took her dancing in a small place in the Valley, and even though it was a respectable place, there was still a lot of drinking going on and she felt uncomfortable. Besides, dancing with Aaron Steele was turning her legs into marshmallows. He held her close and much tighter than he should have, and the feel of the length of his lean, hard body pressed against hers was starting up feelings in Bethany that she knew she had to control. Now and then his lips brushed against her ear, creating havoc throughout her entire body.

When the song ended, she cleared her throat nervously. "Maybe we could—sit down for a while?"

"I have a better idea," he said. "Come on."

Bewildered, she let him lead her to the door. On the

way out, she noticed several people straining their eyes in the dimly lighted place to see if that was really Aaron Steele or simply someone who looked like him.

Driving into the Hollywood Hills, they wound up a narrow road and into a driveway of a moderately large home, partly hidden from view by a line of palm trees along the front. He turned off the ignition.

"What's this?" she asked in astonishment.

"It's where I live. Like it?"

"Your place? We're going inside?"

"No, I thought we'd sit out here in the car and look at it from the driveway. Certainly we're going inside! Come on!"

"Wait," she said, trying to keep her voice calm. Her emotions were in complete turmoil. "Aaron, I just can't. I'm sorry. I really am."

He ran a slender finger down the side of her cheek. "Look, Beth. I'm very tired. I've had a long day. I honestly don't think I'm capable of—of anything. All I want to do is show you my house and sit with you a while. I'm not going to try anything, I promise."

"But—"

"Beth, I said I promise."

The house was complete and total charm, all done in Spanish motif. It suited him perfectly.

He lit a fire in the fireplace, then fixed some coffee and placed the tray down on a coffee table. They sat down on a sofa in front of the fire and Bethany felt peaceful and relaxed. At length, she placed her empty cup in the coffee table and leaned back, closing her eyes.

"I like it here, Aaron. It's just lovely."

"Thank you. It's quiet."

"Yes."

"I have a cleaning lady that comes in during the day to tidy up, but she doesn't live here. I like to come home at night alone and relax without having someone chattering at me."

A confirmed bachelor, she thought dismally, then wondered why that thought should depress her so much. Surely she would never entertain the idea of marrying Aaron Steele! Not that he would ever want to marry her! If he ever did marry, it would most likely be to someone like Vivian Gordon. She could see their picture, adorning all the movie magazines— heads together, love-sick expressions on their faces, the picture probably inside a heart-shaped frame of roses and violets.

A large hand closed around hers, and her eyes snapped open.

"Relax," he said.

She relaxed once more.

For a long time they sat like that, her hand in his, the only sound in the room being the crackling of the fire. Her eyelids were heavy. How easy it would be to sleep, she thought, she was so at ease.

"Beth," he whispered.

She opened her eyes and met his. He was only inches away.

"You're really beautiful," he said.

She blushed, knowing full well that she could never be called beautiful.

As if anticipating an argument, he added, "Yes, you are. I can't describe it, but you have a beauty that seems to come from inside. Maybe it's from God."

"Maybe it is," she replied hopefully.

He kissed her before she could turn away. His

hands slid down over her back and drew her close to him. For a few moments she became caught up in the passion of the moment and her arms wound around his neck, savoring his hungry kisses.

Then sanity returned.

"Aaron. Please."

"Please make love to you?"

She blushed profusely. "No! I mean—please stop."

"Why?"

She looked at him in amazement, realizing how different their worlds were. "I can't, Aaron."

"You wanted me a minute ago, I could tell that. You want me as much as I want you. Don't deny that."

She couldn't deny it. She did want him. "God—God doesn't want me to," she whispered.

He vented an exasperated sigh. "What's so wrong with it? It's just natural—"

"No," she interrupted. "The world may think so, but God—"

"Where are we supposed to be, on Mars?"

"What?"

"You said 'world' like we weren't even on planet Earth."

"I meant that I'm in the world, but I'm not supposed to be a part of worldly things, Aaron."

He raked his fingers through his hair. "You're talking in circles, Beth. What have you used as an excuse before?"

"I—haven't needed any."

He looked at her in surprise. "Do you mean to tell me that you're still a . . ."

She lowered her eyes. "Yes."

56

"Why? Who are you saving it for?"

"The man I will someday marry. That's what God wants me to do, Aaron."

He was quiet a moment, and she wondered if he even heard her. "If you're afraid I would hurt you, I wouldn't, you know. I'd be very gentle with you."

Dear God! Didn't he understand anything she said? Was there nothing that would discourage him?

Apparently he misunderstood her silence for a change of heart. "Come here, honey. Let me hold you—kiss you."

"No, Aaron."

"Come on, Beth."

"Aaron?"

"What?"

"You promised."

She had struck a nerve. He stiffened and it was a moment before he answered her. "You're right. I did. I forgot."

"I'm sorry, Aaron."

"I know you are." His voice was gentle. "Come here and just sit close to me a while, then I'll take you home." She hesitated. "It's OK, Beth. I did promise."

She leaned against the hardness of his chest, and he put his arm around her shoulder. Kissing the top of her head, she barely heard him whisper, "Oh, my dear. My dear, dear, Beth."

A chill caused her to open her eyes. The fire had gone out. But how was that possible when it was blazing away just minutes before? Unless more than just minutes had passed?

She rubbed at the gooseflesh on her arms and

57

nudged Aaron and he opened his eyes. "Aaron, I think we fell asleep. What time is it?"

He blinked his eyes sleepily and looked at his watch. "Two-thirty."

"Two-thirty?" she echoed in alarm.

He yawned and stretched. "I'll take you right home, Beth. I must have been tired."

"Of course you were. You had a long day. I can't imagine why I dozed off though, except that I was so relaxed."

He helped her on with her coat. "Come on. I just hope Frank isn't waiting for me with a baseball bat."

It was still raining but not as hard. They got in the car and he started to back down the driveway, but just as they reached the street, Bethany could see another car coming up the narrow road, approaching at a rapid speed.

"Watch out," she warned. "Here comes a car."

Aaron hit the brakes quickly and the other car screeched to a stop just a short distance from them, its headlights shining directly in her window. She squinted her eyes at the glare. For a second or two the other driver hesitated, then backed up and swerved around Aaron's car and disappeared up the hill.

"Oh, swell," he said. "I'm sure I'll hear all about this."

"Why? Do you know who that was?"

"I sure do. That was a neighbor of mine. Vivian Gordon."

Bethany attended church with the McKenzies Sunday morning and the pastor's sermon was so interesting and dynamic she concentrated fully on what he was saying. But on the way home she thought again of the night before and the tone of Aaron's voice when he realized Vivian Gordon had spotted them leaving his house at two-thirty in the morning. He seemed concerned. Maybe he and the gorgeous actress were more than just friends and co-workers.

Then she remembered something the pastor had said in his sermon that morning. "Abstain from all appearance of evil."

Even though nothing had happened within the walls of Aaron's house that Bethany had cause to be ashamed over, the "appearance" of the two of them leaving at that hour of the morning was surely something Vivian could be suspicious about. Since Vivian was cast in the role of Martha, the sister of Mary and Lazarus, they would destined to meet before too long, and Bethany hoped they wouldn't start out with ill feelings.

Later in the day Frank left with Timothy to go to the market and Bethany and Nora were alone.

"I came home pretty late last night, Nora. I guess you're aware of that."

"We sleep soundly, Beth, but I think I did hear you come in. All I know is that it was past midnight."

"It was two-thirty."

"It was? I mean. . . . Listen, Beth, you don't have to tell me this."

"I know, but I wanted to explain. We went to his house." As Nora's eyebrows lifted, she continued quickly. "We just had some coffee and talked. But he was so tired, and I was so relaxed we fell asleep!"

"Oh, that happened to Frank and me once."

"It did?"

"Yes. When we were dating. My dad was really

59

strict with me, and I had to be home by midnight or I guess I may have turned into a pumpkin or something. Anyway, Frank had been working out of town during the week and coming in one weekends, and we just crammed every minute of the weekends he was here like we'd never see each other again, do you know what I mean?"

"Yes."

"Well, we had gone to a late movie one Sunday evening and Frank had to drive back that night and I was concerned because he was so tired. We were both burned out. But, of course, he was a lot younger then and he could take it. Now I would never let him drive all night." She laughed. "Anyway, he got me home at quarter to twelve, and we were just saying good night when we both fell asleep. The next thing we knew, there was a banging on the car window, and our eyelids flew open to see my dad's angry face. Boy, was he mad! It was one-thirty."

"Oh, no! What did he do?"

"He wouldn't let me see Frank for two weeks. I thought I was going to die."

"I'll bet. Well, I know what you went through."

"Yes. Except that you didn't have an angry father banging on the car window."

"No. Only headlights."

"What?"

"We were backing out of his driveway to let a car pass. The headlights of the other car shone on my window, and I'm sure were every bit as effective as a spot light. Guess who it was?"

"Who?"

"Vivian Gordon."

"Really? The actress?"

"Yes. She's a neighbor of Aaron's. He said he would probably hear about it, so I would imagine Vivian is the jealous type."

"So? You didn't do anything for her to be jealous about, Beth."

"I know that. And Aaron knows that. And God knows that. But Vivian doesn't. To her it looked bad, and you heard what the pastor said this morning about that."

"Yes, you're right."

"I'm not sure what to do about it."

"Well, maybe you won't see her for awhile, and by that time it will all have been forgotten."

She sighed. "I hope you're right."

The opportunity for Bethany to meet Vivian Gordon came sooner than expected.

Calvin called Monday morning with an invitation to go to the studio where they would be shooting "Agape, John" to see some of the sets already being constructed. A half hour after she accepted Cal's invitation, Aaron called.

"Hi! I have the day off today, Beth. Let's spend the day together, OK?"

"Oh! Well, Aaron, I'm sorry, but—"

"Cal again?"

"Uh—well, he asked me to go to the studio to see some of the sets being constructed for 'Agape, John.'"

"I see."

"I'm sorry Aaron, it's just—"

"No problem. Catch you later." And he hung up. His obvious annoyance that she was seeing Cal, bothered her.

She felt sad as Cal drove her to the studio, wishing that Aaron would understand her better. She had promised Cal she would go to the studio with him. Aaron, of all people, should understand the meaning of a promise.

Cal took her to lunch at the studio commissary, then for a tour of some of the other stages where various films were being shot. When they arrived at the sound stage where her play would be filmed, men were busily at work, constructing the fronts of buildings along a narrow street. At one end was an arch, typical of the entrance into a city in the Holy Land, and she had to touch the large stones before she could believe they weren't cut from solid rock. No doubt they would be using this set for a number of scenes, one of which would be early in the play when the Apostle John asked Jesus to call fire down upon the Samaritans for their unbelief, earning him and his brother the nickname, "Sons of Thunder." She continued to stand in awe, watching the creation of a replica of a place where Jesus once walked.

"Looking pretty good, wouldn't you say so?" Cal asked.

"Oh, yes!" she exclaimed. "I can't believe how real it looks!"

"Any suggestions you can think of?"

She looked at a high roof being thrown over a portion of the street, and the close lattice work in the windows of the upper rooms. "None at this point. Really, I'm amazed, Cal."

"Oh, there's Mike. Will you excuse me for just a minute, Beth?"

"Go right ahead," she replied. "I'll just wait here. I'm too busy gawking!"

Bethany watched in fascination as the carpenters and painters continued to add detail to the set. It was amazing how fast they worked and how accurate they were in the reproduction. She was so preoccupied with what was going on that she didn't hear at first, an icy, feminine voice speaking to her, apparently, for the second time.

"I asked you, how well do you know Aaron?"

Bethany turned to face the beautiful and sultry expression of Vivian Gordon. At the moment, the woman's breath-taking features wore a stormy expression. "Oh! Excuse me for not answering you right away," Bethany said as pleasantly as she could. "I was so fascinated by all of this." She indicated the set with a sweep of her arm. The actress remained unmoved by any excuses and Bethany's arm dropped to her side. "Aaron and I met only a few days ago, Miss Gordon. We've been working together on the script."

The actress' eyes narrowed. "You're the writer of the play, aren't you?"

Bethany smiled. "Yes."

"And you say you and Aaron have been working together?"

"Yes, that's correct."

"Until two-thirty in the morning? At *his* house? *Alone* together?"

Bethany's face flushed pink. Just the thought of what Vivian Gordon was implying was embarrassing, and no doubt the instantaneous blush added to the actress' suspicions. Yet Bethany's voice remained calm. "I know how that must have looked to you, but nothing happened, really. It's not what you're thinking. We fell asleep in front of the fire."

Vivian laughed. "Fell asleep? *Aaron*? Hardly!"

Bethany blushed again. The human side of her wanted to slap the face of this lovely brunette for her implications and her rudeness. But Bethany yielded to the leading of the Holy Spirit. "I know how it must have looked at that hour, Miss Gordon, and for that reason and the fact that you don't know me, you have every right to think what you're thinking. I suppose I can expect your accusations because the Bible teaches us to abstain from all appearance of evil and I certainly didn't. I feel I should apologize if I've caused you any hurt feelings. But you must believe me. Nothing went on between Aaron and me."

The actress placed graceful hands on nicely rounded hips and stared at Bethany. "If you think I'm going to stand here and swallow that line of bull—"

"Hold it, Vivian!"

They both turned to the sound of the masculine voice. Though Bethany was happy to see Aaron and grateful for his intervention, she was bothered by what he must have heard and felt remorse that his reputation was being questioned because of her.

"Beth is absolutely right," he said. "Nothing happened." He took a step closer to Vivian and looked her in the eyes defiantly. "Not that I didn't want it to," he added.

Vivian spun on her high heels and walked away without another word, and Bethany was left gaping at Aaron.

He smiled gently at Bethany. "You'll have to excuse Vivian," he said. "She can be pretty ruthless at times."

"Well, she saw us leave your place the other night, Aaron. She had every reason to think what she did. I'm really sorry."

"You have no reason to apologize." He took hold of her hands and smiled down at her. "You're amazing!" he said. "How could you possibly remain so controlled and calm and even polite to her? I've heard other women really tell her off! You didn't even swear at her!"

"Swear at her? I should hope not!"

He shook his head. "You're remarkable!" he said.

"I'm not remarkable," she replied gently. "But God is."

His smile faded a little and he studied her with an enigmatic expression. He appeared to be searching for the right words and unable to come up with anything he considered appropriate. Finally, he turned to the work in progress around them. "What do you think, Beth? Like it?"

"Oh, yes! I was just telling Cal how real it looks!"

He looked around. "Where is Cal? did he desert you?"

"No, he excused himself a minute to talk to Mike Innes. I'm not sure where they went," she said.

"I can take you home if he's going to be tied up," he said hopefully.

"Thank you, but I'm certain he'll be back in a moment. He said something about dinner."

"He's taking you to dinner?"

"Yes."

He sighed in exasperation. "What about tomorrow night? I know of a great Italian restaurant—"

"No, not tomorrow night."

"Cal again?" he asked sarcastically.

"No, not Cal," she answered patiently. "There's a Bible study group at the house. Won't you come to it? I'd love to have you there!"

65

"I'll pass on that, thanks!"

She tried to hide her disappointment. "It won't last too long, Aaron. I mean, if you have an early call Wednesday, or something." *Please, God!*

"We still have lots to talk about, you know," he said sulkily. "About the play."

"Yes, I know." *Please, Lord?*

"If the Bible study doesn't last too long, could we talk afterward?"

Her face shone. *Thank you, God!* "Yes, of course!"

"OK, what time?"

"Seven-thirty, and just wear jeans if you want. Nora said no one dresses up." She looked up at him and smiled her brightest smile.

He simply nodded and she couldn't be sure if his expression meant uncertainty at what he was getting himself into or remorse that he had been too hasty in his agreement to attend the Bible study.

Please Lord, let it be a blessing to him!

CHAPTER 5

GLENN DAVIDSON ARRIVED EARLY Tuesday night, which gave Bethany a chance to get acquainted with him. It was difficult for her to imagine that he had ever been anything but a child of God, so radiant and sweet was the expression in his eyes. He had been out jogging and still wore his sweats and in talking to him, Bethany learned he only lived three blocks from the McKenzies. He was a tall, well-built man with a well-trimmed beard and wavy, brown hair. How wonderful that he had accepted the Lord, she thought, before appearing in the play! How much more convincing his role would be now, as Jesus Christ!

The rest of the group arrived on time or a few minutes early. One couple brought their four-year-old son and Timothy promptly took charge and led the smaller boy to his room to play.

An older man brought his guitar. His smile was so captivating that Bethany scarcely noticed he was completely bald. Everyone was friendly and laughing and at ease, and when Aaron arrived, Bethany thought at first it might present a problem, in that his presence would be a distraction to the Bible study. But her apprehensions were unfounded, and Aaron was swept into the group as though he had always belonged. He was invited to sit next to the man with the guitar.

After Frank led the group in prayer, they sang three or four songs with guitar accompaniment before the study began. Bethany glanced at Aaron when they were singing, and he seemed uncomfortable since he apparently only knew the words to one song, which was a standard hymn. He even jumped a little when a woman sitting on the other side of him lifted her hands in praise during the singing of one of the songs.

The man with the guitar, whose name was Dan, led the study and began by asking everyone to turn to Chapter 13 of First Corinthians. Since Aaron brought no Bible with him, the lady next to him shared hers. Dan began to read the familiar passage of Scripture from a newer translation.

" 'Love is patient and kind; love is not jealous, or conceited or proud; love is not ill-mannered, or selfish, or irritable; love does not keep a record of wrongs; love is not happy with evil, but is happy with the truth. Love never gives up: its faith, hope, and patience never fail.' " He paused and looked around. "Anyone care to comment or elaborate on that?" he asked.

"I thank God He's given me the capacity to love," Glenn replied softly. "I wasn't able to before."

"Love is at the very heart of Christianity," Nora said. "Look at verse 13. Paul said it's the greatest of the Christian virtues."

"I'm with Glenn," Frank commented. "Before I knew Jesus, I had no ability to love. Not like the Bible teaches anyway. Turn to 1 John, Chapter 4," he said. "This is love, the Bible says in verse 10. 'Not that we have loved God, but that He loved us and sent His Son to be the means by whom our sins are forgiven.'"

Aaron smiled a little in recognition of some of the words since Bethany had used the Scriptures in the play. She prayed that he would be able to look at them in a fresh light and give the lines a whole new meaning.

Throughout the discussion of "love" Aaron said nothing. He didn't look impatient or bored, for which Bethany was grateful, but from time to time he had a puzzled expression on his face. He remained a mute but polite witness to what was going on around him, and it wasn't until the Bible study was over and Nora served coffee and cookies that he indulged in conversation with those sitting near him.

It was impossible for Bethany to keep her eyes off him; he looked so incredibly handsome. He wore well-fitting jeans and a soft sweater of icy aqua blue, which seemed to be a perfect color for him. Adoringly, she watched as he chatted with those around him, his face serious at times or breaking into a grin when someone said something humorous.

It didn't take long for the truth to sink into her consciousness. She was in love with Aaron Steele.

A helpless kind of feeling washed over her. Right now there was nothing she could do about it. Their lives were just too different for any hope of compatibility.

When he looked up and caught her eyes, she inadvertently blushed. His eyebrows lifted questioningly but she realized it wasn't because of what he had read in her expression, only that he was silently inquiring of her if this would be an appropriate time to leave.

Bethany stood up and turned to Nora. "Would you excuse Aaron and me?" she asked. "We do have a lot of things to discuss about the play."

"Of course!" Nora replied with a grin. Several of the group, including Dan, gave Bethany a brief, but warm embrace, and they all invited both her and Aaron to return.

He seemed a little taken back by the open display of affection, but it wasn't until they were in his car that he commented on it.

"I can't say that I appreciated all those hugs you were given," he said rather peevishly. "Especially by the men. Is that customary?"

"Those were Holy hugs," she replied with a smile.

"They were what?"

"Holy hugs. That's what my father always calls a Christian embrace," she said gently. "Anyway, Paul said in many of his epistles to greet one another with a Holy kiss. It's an expression of Christian love."

He started the ignition. "And that's another thing I don't understand, Beth. All that talk about love. What was it Dan read? Oh, yes, the part about love not being jealous. Does that mean that if I'm jealous of Calvin Bruce I don't know the true meaning of love?"

Bethany's heart leaped. *Why did he ask that?* she wondered. Was he indirectly telling her he loved her? No, that was a ridiculous assumption! He was asking a hypothetical question. She swallowed hard, trying to keep her voice steady and still the momentary excitement that had just traveled through her. "I—I don't know if you have knowledge of the true meaning of love, Aaron," she said. "Only God knows that. But as for being jealous—well, it's wrong but it's a difficult emotion to control."

"Are you ever jealous?"

She reddened a little, remembering the jealousy she had for him and Vivian Gordon. "I—I suppose so, at times."

"But you're a Christian! You're not supposed to be, are you?"

"Christians aren't perfect, Aaron."

"I see. Recently?"

"What?"

"Have you been jealous recently?"

"Uh—excuse me Aaron, but where are we going?"

Her swift change in the topic of conversation served to distract him from his interrogation. "Beats me. I'm just driving. We do have a problem, you know."

"What kind of a problem?"

"A problem of where to go to talk! I don't suppose we could go to my place?"

"It would be better if we didn't. I mean, it isn't right, Aaron. Besides, if Vivian ever saw us again . . ."

"Ah, yes! Vivian!"

Bethany wasn't certain how he meant that, whether it was in exasperation or admiration. She chose to let it pass. "We could drive to the beach again," she suggested. "It's awfully pretty there, by the sea."

"Yes, it is. But it looks like it's going to rain again. Sure you won't be cold?"

"No, I'm fine."

"You could sit a little closer to me, Beth." She moved a little nearer to him, and he put one arm around her shoulder. When she tensed, he chuckled. "You really are skittish, aren't you? I never saw anything like it! Well, relax, dear. I certainly won't force myself on you."

Watching the waves crashing into the shore had a soothing effect on Bethany. But Aaron felt something else in the fierceness of the raging sea.

"There's a bad storm coming. I can see it in those waves out there."

"Really? How bad can it get?"

"Pretty bad. See those little homes near the shore?"

Bethany turned to look. She didn't think they looked so little, but she nodded. "Yes. What about them?"

"Sometimes a storm can become so violent the waves will crash against those dwellings and do severe damage. Sometimes they can even be completely wrecked—washed right into the sea."

"Oh, no! Do you think that's likely to happen this time?"

"I don't know. Only God knows that, I suppose." Then he chuckled again. "Listen to me! I'm starting to sound like Bethany Jordan!"

She smiled. How wonderful it was to hear him refer to the omniscience of God.

He was quiet a moment before he spoke again. "Beth, all that talk of love still bothers me. I thought I knew all about love."

"And now you have doubts?"

"I don't know. It's something I have to wrestle with, I guess. I know the lines toward the end of the play are almost all about love, but . . ."

"But what?"

"I'm just hoping I can grab the viewer's attention. The TV audience has command, you know. With one flip of a switch, they can turn you right out into the ozone."

"They won't. You'll be good as John. I just know it."

He eyed her shrewdly. "You seem to have a lot of confidence in me. I hope you're right."

She smiled. "I know I am!"

"You've certainly written a winner. The characters are all well-fleshed out, and it should be fairly easy to get the audience to respond in a way that they see the characters living out their lives."

"Thank you."

"But it still takes good acting!"

"You are a good actor!"

"I know! But I have to believe what I'm doing is right."

"And?"

"And that reminds me," he said. "What about this character change in John?"

"What don't you understand, Aaron?"

"It doesn't make sense," he said. "All through the beginning of the play John is strong and outspoken. Suddenly, he's like a different person."

"He is a different person, spiritually."

"But his character—"

"He's still strong and outspoken, Aaron. Only in a different way."

"He's different."

"Exactly."

"It doesn't make sense."

"It does make sense. He met Jesus. Jesus changed him. It's as simple as that."

"It isn't simple. Nobody changes like that."

"Glenn Davidson did."

"Oh, Glenn! He's just on the wagon for a few days! Give him time and he'll go off on a drunk again!"

"Maybe not, Aaron."

"Come on! You can't tell me he's changed that much and that fast! I only hope he stays sober while we're shooting!"

Back to square one, she thought in frustration.

"Let's get back to the subject of love," he said. "Frank said tonight he had no ability to love before he met Jesus. Surely he was in love with Nora?"

"I'm sure he was in love with his wife," Bethany replied patiently. "But that's not what he meant."

"No? What about making love? I suppose that's not what he meant either?"

She flushed. "No—"

"Come here," he said, drawing her close to him. "I don't think I need to learn any more about making love. I just wish you'd change your mind and let me show you."

"Aaron—"

He cupped her chin, tilting her face to his, and kissed her. Bethany closed her eyes and responded to his kiss, allowing him to envelope her in his arms, yielding to the way he was caressing her hair, her shoulders.

"Beth," he whispered, "come back to my house with me."

"No, Aaron. It's best that we don't."

"Don't you care for me? A little?"

His question surprised her. "Of course I do! Do you think I would be sitting here like this, letting you kiss me, if I didn't?"

"Then come back with me."

"No."

"You want to, though. Don't you?"

She hesitated. "The human part of me does, yes, but the spiritual side—"

He let go of her and started the ignition. "Here we go again," he said with an exasperated sigh. "I guess it's time I took you home, Beth. It's starting to rain."

The next morning, Bethany awoke to the sound of a downpour outside. The deluge was coming down in great sheets of water, splashing with tremendous force against her windows and drenching everything in sight.

She slid out of bed and into a robe, then washed her face and brushed her hair. When she padded to the kitchen, she was surprised to find that Frank had already left for work.

"You were sleeping so soundly I just let you sleep on," Nora said, pouring her a cup of coffee. "I hope that was OK."

Bethany brushed a strand of hair from her eyes and yawned. "Oh, sure." She glanced at the clock. "Nine o'clock? Well, I probably needed that sleep. Oh, no!" Her eyes fell to the open newspaper on the kitchen table and she was startled to read that three homes along the beach had suffered severe damage from the storm. "Aaron was right!" she exclaimed.

"About what?"

"The storm! How terrible!"

Nora glanced at the paper. "Oh, yes! Isn't it? I'm glad no lives were lost, though." She looked out the window. "Looks like this one may be with us a while, Beth." Then she grinned. "Oh, well, it takes both rain and sunshine to make a rainbow, so they say!"

Nora scooped some pancakes off the griddle onto a plate and placed it in front of Bethany. "There's some maple syrup on the table. Can I get you anything else?"

"Goodness no! Gee, I could have helped myself, Nora, but thank you! I'm not sure if I can eat all of this, but I'll sure give it a good try!" She bowed her head in silent prayer and Nora waited respectfully until she finished. She began to dig into the pancakes, hungrier than she thought she was.

Nora sat at the table with her and sipped her coffee. "I really like Aaron," she said.

Bethany grinned. "Me too!"

"I'll bet! What did he think of the Bible study?"

"He was interested. Confused."

"I'm glad he was interested. What was confusing to him?"

"The whole subject of love, actually. His idea of love centers around the physical. It's hard for him to understand the love of God."

"It's hard for any nonbeliever to understand that," Nora said. "Beth, it's none of my business, but is he making things difficult for you?"

"In what way?"

"Well, you mentioned physical love—"

"Oh, I see what you mean." Bethany smiled. "At times it is difficult, Nora, because I really feel strongly toward him. And this may sound silly to you but I— I'm in love with him."

"That doesn't sound silly. I fell in love with Frank on our first date!"

"Really?"

"Yes. Frank didn't, though. At least he didn't think so! I had to work hard to convince him he was in love with me, too! He finally admitted that he loved me all along!'' They both laughed. ''And Aaron—how does he feel?''

''I'm not sure.. I know he's attracted to me. And I know he wants to make love to me. But I've never known a man in that way, and I want to wait until I'm married.''

''Did you tell him that?''

''Yes.''

''And?''

''It's hard for him to accept that, Nora.''

''I can see where it would be. Wouldn't it be something if he proposed marriage?'' she asked excitedly.

Bethany sighed. ''That's not likely to happen. Anyway that's not the thing that bothers me the most. I'm praying really hard that God will open his eyes to the meaning of agape love, so that he'll be able to cope with the last scenes in the play. He's really wrestling with the lines now, and I feel sorry for him.''

Nora reached across the table and patted her hand. ''I'll pray, too. We'll all pray about that,'' she said. ''And remember the verse, 'Fear not, stand still, and see the salvation of the Lord.' ''

''Oh, Nora! I've felt impressed to lean on the promise of that verse, too. I guess we'll have to give it to Him, won't we?''

Nora nodded. ''Best thing to do.'' She poured Bethany another cup of coffee. ''Was Aaron uncomfortable about anything else last night?''

''Well, he was a little huffy about all the hugging,'' she said with a giggle. She took a sip of coffee. ''Actually, I'm amazed that everyone acted so normal.''

"Normal?"

"Yes, with Aaron Steele. No one reacted to him like I thought they would to a rather well-known film personality. Is that because here in Los Angeles, everyone is used to it?"

"Partly. I'm sure people here don't ogle movie stars like they do in other states. There are too many instances where the movie actors and actresses are seen in normal surroundings, like at Disneyland, a department store, a supermarket. They're just people doing a job, even though the job is more glamorous than most. There's another reason, though, why people last night acted normal, as you put it."

"What's that?"

"I called them up ahead of time and told them to!"

Bethany laughed. "No wonder! It was great, though, because I know he was concerned about that beforehand. It sure would have been different back home. I can see them all now, sitting there with open Bibles and open mouths and no one saying a word!"

Nora laughed, then grew serious. "Do you miss your family, Beth?"

"Yes, I really do. But you and Frank and Timothy are next best!"

"Why don't you call home? I'm sure that would be a welcome relief from a letter, wouldn't it?"

"Oh, yes! I really would appreciate that, Nora. I'll reimburse you for the call."

"You don't have to. Only if it would make you feel better. Go right ahead!"

Bethany was about to pick up the receiver when the phone rang and she jumped. She answered it. "Hello?"

"Nora?"

"No, just a minute."

"Wait! Is this Beth?"

"Yes. Cal? Is that you?"

He chuckled. "Yes. Sorry about that. Actually it's you I want to talk to. I just didn't expect you to answer the phone."

"I was right by it!"

"Oh, well, I have news."

"You do? What kind?"

"Good kind. They're going to start shooting 'Agape, John' next week, beginning with the scene where Lazarus is brought back to life. Have you finished with the rewrite of the first part of that scene?"

"Yes, I have. Actually, I don't have much more to do on any of it at this point."

"You probably will. But if you run out of things to keep you busy, don't worry, honey! I have plenty for you to do!"

She laughed good-naturedly. "I'm sure you do! Want to tell me about it?"

"Yes, but not over the phone. How about having dinner with me tonight?"

She hesitated. What if Aaron were to call? She argued with herself. What if he did? She was not obligated after all, it was strictly business between her and Cal.

"Beth? Are you there?"

"What? Oh! Yes, Cal. Dinner will·be fine!"

Her evening with Calvin Bruce was pleasant and relaxing. Cal was good company and a very kind and considerate man. All through dinner he talked excitedly about his plans for her concerning the continuation of plays written around biblical characters.

When Beth suggested focusing on an outstanding woman as well as the men, of the Old or New Testament, he hesitated at first. But when she reminded him of all the possibilities such as Sarah, Rachel, and Miriam, sister of Moses, in the Old Testament, and Mary Magdalene, Elizabeth, mother of John the Baptist, and others in the New Testament, he became enthused. The whole evening was an inspiration to both of them, and Bethany could scarcely wait to begin writing on a new play.

The only damper on the evening was when she returned to the house and learned that Aaron had called in her absence and Frank had to tell him she was out with Calvin Bruce.

There was no further word from Aaron the rest of the week. Bethany managed to plunge into her writing, inspired by the encouragement she had received from Cal. But from time to time her mind would center on Aaron Steele, the man she had grown to love, and she would begin to wonder where he was, what he was doing, whom he was with.

And the continued rain only reminded her of her own tears, bottled up and swelling inside, which she refused to release.

CHAPTER 6

IN SPITE OF THE disappointment Bethany felt over not hearing from Aaron, she still was hopeful and optimistic over certain things in her life that had become important to her.

She was optimistic about a new script she was working on. She had decided to write about Miriam. So many stories had been done about Moses, Bethany felt it would be good to center a play around his sister. She would of course, begin with Miriam watching after her baby brother, so carefully hidden by their mother. And there could be a marvelous scene after the Israelites crossed the Red Sea and Miriam led the women in singing and dancing with timbrels. Miriam's song of praise could be elaborated upon and proper music written for it. One of the dramatic moments would occur later on when Miriam criticized Moses for marrying a Cushite woman and received the Lord's punishment of leprosy. There were so many possibilities! Bethany tingled with excitement!

Images of characters were darting through her brain and snatches of dialogue flashed at her in an almost elusive manner throughout the day. Bethany had jotted these inspirations down as they played on her mind until she filled the little notebook she carried with her and had also a quantity of little scribbled-on slips of paper stuffed in one of her suitcases.

She had spent most of the day Friday going through these notes and letting them take shape. She was beginning to see structure now—rough sketches of her new play. It was wonderful!

The writing also helped distract her from the absence of any call from Aaron. Yet, she had hope for him. Hope that he would soon learn that love in its true reality and power, is seen in the bond uniting all the Christian virtues.

Whether God had plans for her and Aaron she did not know, but even if they would eventually go their separate ways, Bethany's prayers were that Aaron would enter into a personal relationship with Jesus. And as much as she loved him, she could be content without him, with God's help, just knowing that he had the Lord in his life.

Momentarily, she pulled her thoughts away from Aaron and held in retrospect the pleasant conversation she had with her parents over the phone. Pangs of homesickness shot through her and she thought of the many reminders she had of her parents and her life back home resulting from that phone call. She missed a lot of things. She missed the clean, crisp air. And the farm and ranch animals.

Soon it would be calving time, the time when those precious little animals would be brought into the world, shivering in the February cold, then warmed by their mothers. She could picture the babies lying on their straw beds, the cows licking them tenderly, and how, just moments after they were born, the little calves would be up and running around. It was a particularly tender time of the year for Bethany.

She thought of the Cramer's ranch near her home and the gentle chestnut mare she was allowed to ride. How good it would feel now, to climb on the back of that sweet horse and ride! She recalled how that mare really liked to run and what a smooth ride they would have, going like the wind! And the animal loved it when they were moving at a leisurely pace and Bethany would sing. The mare's ears would go back as though she were trying to hear better and at times Bethany was convinced that the horse's steps were in time to the music!

No one could ever convince Bethany that horses were not intelligent creatures. She recalled one time at the Cramer's ranch when she was leaning against the fence of the paddock that housed her favorite mare, and talking to Mrs. Cramer. The horse kept coming over to Bethany and nudging her shoulder, then running off to the other end of the paddock.

When the horse repeated this about three times, Mrs. Cramer said, "I think she's trying to show you something."

Bethany realized that the nudge of the animal's nose against her shoulder was an attempt to turn her around. When she faced the other way, the mare again went to the opposite end of the paddock.

"Let's go and see what she wants," Mrs. Cramer suggested.

When they got to where the horse was standing, they found an accumulation of leaves clogging the automatic water trough and the mare was unable to get a drink of water! Bethany removed the leaves and the animal got her drink, then nodded her great head at Bethany as if to say, "Thanks!"

She smiled at the pleasant memory.

She liked Los Angeles, but she still missed her home. She couldn't help but wonder if God was going to send her back there or keep her here.

Plans to spend Saturday at Disneyland were shelved because of the still-inclement weather, and Bethany was even more disappointed than Timothy. She had never been to Disneyland and was looking forward to it ever since Nora and Frank invited her to go along. But Timothy consoled her in an almost adult manner.

"There'll be other days, Bethany. Disneyland's no fun when it's raining."

She stayed with Timothy while Nora and Frank went shopping and the two of them played a simple game, for a while at least, until one of his friends came over and the two little boys ran into Timothy's room to play.

Three times she went to the phone and touched the receiver, tempted to call Aaron. But each time she withdrew her hand after a moment's hesitation.

She would wait.

Bethany knew she would see Vivian Gordon again at the studio so it was difficult for her to explain the strange feelings of apprehension she felt when she came face to face with the woman on Monday. Vivian was in costume for her role as Martha. She gave Bethany a cool "hello" then turned and headed in the opposite direction. She appeared to be looking for someone. Aaron Steele, most probably, Bethany thought sourly.

Bethany found a chair in an inconspicuous corner of the stage where she could observe but not be in the way. She was again in awe at the realistic scene before her—the home of Mary and Martha, the tomb of Lazarus a distance away, with a large stone in front of the opening.

She had to admit that Vivian looked lovely. And quite appropriately dressed for the part. And so was Glenn Davidson. It was amazing to her how convincing he seemed in his role.

He wandered over to where she was sitting and sat down next to her.

"Hi, Beth! Enjoying yourself?"

"Yes! Just looking at it is a thrill!"

"How does it feel to be successful and famous?"

She laughed. "Oh, please! I'm not, yet!"

"You will be. I just know this play will be a good one. And your career will take off like a rocket!"

"Well—just so my work pleases God."

"It will."

Someone called to Glenn. He excused himself, and Bethany heard voices behind her.

Standing a few feet away were Aaron and Vivian. Aaron had his back to Bethany, but the sultry actress saw her. She gave an almost feline smile and then turned to Aaron.

"Do you want me to come over again tonight, darling?" she asked.

"Well, if you can, Vivian. You know I'd appreciate it."

"It's obvious you need me, love."

"Well . . ."

Her slender arms moved up and wound around his neck, and she cooed, "Mm—you know how willing I am to please you, Aaron."

"So it seems."

"And your place is so cozy and warm by the fire."

Bethany felt sick to her stomach. She could listen to no more. Standing on trembling legs, she walked away, still unseen by Aaron Steele.

CHAPTER 7

THE NEXT DAY BETHANY woke up with a sore throat and a headache. She couldn't decide whether it was from the day before when she had let Vivian's disgusting words to Aaron get to her or whether she really had the flu.

She had a glass of juice and skipped the rest of her breakfast, which brought a worried frown to Nora's face.

"Do you feel all right, Beth?"

"No, not really. I have a headache and my throat's sore. And I'm kind of sick to my stomach. I don't think I could keep any breakfast down, Nora."

"I feel a little queasy too, but I don't think it's the flu."

Bethany looked up listlessly. "What?"

Nora smiled. "Never mind."

Bethany stood up from the table. "I think I'll just go and see if I can get some work done."

"Why don't you just rest?"

"I need to work. It—it will be good for me."

Nora shrugged. "OK. But if you want anything, will you let me know?"

"Sure. Thanks, Nora."

She went to her room and sat with her pen poised over a blank piece of paper for a long time before she put the pen down and picked up her Bible.

"Lord," she prayed. "I can't stop thinking about what I heard yesterday. I know it may just be nothing. It may just be Vivian trying to throw cold water on what she thinks is going on between Aaron and me, but . . ." Tears filled her eyes.

She knew that writing would help, if she could get started. It would take her mind off her illness, and off Vivian. And Aaron.

Tenderly, she opened her Bible to her favorite Psalm and read, "The Lord will give strength unto His people; the Lord will bless His people with peace."

An inner calm seemed to take over the moment she read those precious words. Smiling, she lay the Bible to one side and reflected on the countless times a certain passage of Scripture was perfect for the need she had at that moment.

She began to work, strength filling her body and thoughts of Vivian Gordon fading.

Around noon, there was a gentle knock at the door. "Nora?"

"Yes. May I come in?"

"Oh, sure! You don't have to ask!"

Nora came in with a tray. "I didn't want to interrupt you. How's the writing coming?"

"Pretty well."

"Good! Are you feeling any better?"

"I think so. A little."

"Well, that's encouraging. I brought you some hot, chicken soup. Don't laugh," she said when Bethany started to smile, "it really does wonders for the punies." She placed the tray on the desk top.

"Thanks, Nora, but you shouldn't have gone to such a bother. I could have come out to the kitchen!"

"Come on now, be honest! Knowing you, you probably would have stayed right in here, writing."

Bethany grinned. "I suppose you're right!" The soup was hot and rich-tasting and seemed to settle pretty well in her stomach.

Nora sat on the edge of the bed. "The Bible study group meets tonight at a home in the east end of the Valley. Think you'll feel up to it or would you rather stay home and rest?"

"I think I'll pass tonight, Nora. I want to be sure and be over this bug, whatever it is, and maybe if I get a good night's rest it will help."

"I'm sure it would. Anyway, the weather is still pretty cold and damp. It's best not to get out in it."

"I'll be happy to watch Timothy, though."

"Well, thank you, but he can go with us. There are two children there right around his age, and they get along fine."

"Oh. Well, he's probably looking forward to that."

"I'll say he is! They have a playroom you wouldn't believe! It's hard to drag him out of it!"

Bethany laughed. She could picture the three youngsters hauling out every toy in sight.

"Things should be quiet for you here," Nora said. "The only disturbance I can think of that you might have is the paper boy. If he comes to collect, there's money on the table near the front door."

"Oh sure. Fine."

"Want some more soup?"

"No, thanks. That really was good, and I believe it's going to stay down."

"I hope so."

"Nora, did you say earlier you weren't feeling well?"

Nora grinned. "Yes, but I'm fine, now."

"Good. I wouldn't want to think I'd given you my germs."

"Not a chance!" Nora chuckled softly to herself as she removed the tray and Bethany puzzled, not quite sure what was so funny.

After the McKenzies left, Bethany soaked in a warm, relaxing bath, then put on a fleecy bathrobe and slippers. With her hair still pinned up in back of her neck and a light layer of cream smoothed over her face, she padded to the kitchen to fix a cup of hot tea.

She took a china cup and saucer out of the cupboard. There was something about drinking tea out of a mug that was inappropriate for some reason. Maybe it was her mother's influence.

"You can drink coffee out of one of those heavy mugs," her mother would say, "but tea belongs in a china cup." Bethany smiled to herself at how adamant her mother used to get over that.

She had no sooner poured the water into the cup over the tea bag when the doorbell rang. She hurried to the entry hall, picked up the money Nora spoke of for the paper boy, and opened the door.

"Hi! I hope I'm not too late—Oh!" Aaron stood in the doorway, a Bible in his hand and a confused expression on his face.

Bethany wanted to die. She clutched at the neckline of her robe with one hand, pulled at the pins in her hair with the other and wished she could just will the cream to disappear from her beet-red face.

His eyes swept over her, causing the blush on her face to deepen even more. "I guess this isn't the night!" he said with an amused grin.

"Oh. Uh—come in, Aaron. No, this—well yes, it is the night but it isn't here. It's at someone else's house. They rotate."

"Oh. How come you're home?"

"I didn't feel good, so . . ."

He frowned. "Nothing serious, I hope?"

She walked over to the small table and put the money back, depositing a little pile of hairpins on top. "No, no, just a little touch of the flu, I think. I feel a lot better now than I did this morning. Nora gave me some chicken soup."

He laughed. "Does that really work?"

"It seemed to!" she said with a smile. "Oh—listen, uh—here, let me have your coat." She took the smartly tailored jean-jacket and hung it in the hall closet. "Uh—will you sit down and excuse me for just a moment?"

"Sure—go ahead."

She hurried to her room and changed into a pair of jeans and a T-shirt. Then she brushed her hair, wiped the cream from her face and picked up her Bible.

It was then that she realized how foolish she had just been and how vanity had completely taken over. The only thing she had just felt was embarrassment in being "caught" looking a mess by Aaron Steele. Her eyes had been closed to the importance of the moment: Aaron had come over to study the Bible—voluntarily! He had chosen to come and learn more about the word of God. It was surely answered prayer. A lump rose in her throat as she prayed silently, *Forgive me, Lord. And thank you, sweet Jesus.*

Quite suddenly, the way she looked was unimportant. And the words of Vivian Gordon faded into obscurity. The only thing that mattered right at this moment was that Aaron Steele be enlightened through the precious Scriptures.

She was smiling when she returned to the living room. When she saw him sitting on the sofa, his head bent over an open Bible, tears of joy filled her eyes.

He closed the Bible when she came in and smiled up at her, and she blinked away the tears before he could question them.

"Well," he said, "you look fine, but you didn't have to wipe the cream off your face on my account! I've seen women wearing cream on their faces before!"

She momentarily wondered when and where he could have seen women in such intimate attire, then dismissed the thought before it had a negative effect on her.

"My mother, for example," he said with a sagacious wink. "And there's no absence of cold cream at the studio!"

She brightened. "Oh, that's right! Well, as long as you're here for Bible study, I think we should get on with it, what do you say?"

"Do you feel up to it?"

"Sure!"

He shrugged and grinned. "OK. Whatever you say!"

"Want a cup of tea?"

"No, thanks, nothing. But you go ahead if you were going to."

"No, that's OK," she said quickly. She sat down next to him and opened her Bible. "I believe they're studying First John," she said.

"Oh, sure." He fumbled through the book and finally in exasperation, turned to the table of contents. "It's a new Bible," he said, half-offering an apology.

"It's a lovely one," she replied with a smile.

Her answer seemed to put him at ease. "What chapter are we on?" he asked.

"Chapter 5. Do you want to read the first three verses?"

"Oh. Well, OK." He cleared his throat and began reading from the King James. "Whosoever believeth that Jesus is the Christ is born of God: and everyone that loveth Him that begat loveth him also that is begotten of Him." He stopped and vented a deep sigh. "It's no use, Beth. I just don't understand it."

She touched the back of his hand. "You will," she said gently. "First, let's ask God to help you."

He remained quiet as she offered a short prayer for God to give them understanding.

"Now then," she went on, "that passage of Scripture means that if you believe Jesus is the Messiah, you're a child of God. And if you love the Father, you love His children, too. And we show our love for God and His children by obeying His commandments, which are not too difficult, really, for us to do." She pointed to the second and third verses. "See?"

"You make it sound so much easier," he said. "Or maybe I should have bought an easier translation."

"It might have helped. Sometimes it's nice to have two or three translations. That way, one clarifies the other."

"That's a good idea," he said. "OK, you read."

" '. . . every child of God is able to defeat the world. That is how we win the victory over the world: with our faith. Who can defeat the world? Only he who believes that Jesus is the Son of God.' " She looked up at him to see if he was comprehending but apparently he was confused again.

"There's all that about the 'world' again," he said. "Just like you were rattling about the other night. I still don't understand that."

"Look at verse 19," she said.

He read aloud. " 'And we know that we are of God, and the whole world lieth in wickedness.' " He closed his Bible. "Oh, come on. The whole world isn't wicked."

"I think my translation is clearer for that verse. It says, '. . . the whole world is under the rule of the Evil One.' "

"Meaning?"

"Satan."

He shook his head. "Then why did you say the other night you are in the world but not a part of the world?"

"Because I don't belong to Satan."

"Oh." He was silent a moment, seemingly pondering over what she had just said.

"Are you seeing it a little more clearly?" she asked.

"I think so. Maybe."

She brightened. "Then you'll be happy to know that God answered our prayers."

"About what?"

"About giving you understanding. Look here at the last two verses. 'We know that the Son of God has come and has given us understanding, so that we know the true God. Our lives are in the true God, and this is eternal life. My children, keep yourselves safe from false gods.' "

"I see. What false gods?"

"Could be many. Any idol that is worshiped is a false god. Money is a good example."

" 'Money is the root of all evil,' isn't that what the Bible says?" he asked.

"No. It says the *love* of money is the root of all evil. There's a big difference."

"Then it's OK for Christians to be rich?"

"There's nothing wrong with having money. It all comes from God. But you have to use it wisely, the way He wants you to."

He sighed again. "Oh, Beth," he said, leaning his head back. "I thought I was an intelligent man. Yet I seem to know so little about this book."

"Do you want to know more?"

"Certainly I do!"

"Then you will!"

"How can you be sure of that?"

"It's a promise of the Lord! Those who seek after righteousness shall be filled!"

"Well, I'll keep on seeking," he said. He took her hand and squeezed it. "You're such a lovely woman, Beth."

She flushed a little at the unexpected comment and lowered her eyes. "Thank you," she whispered.

"I mean you're lovely on the outside and on the inside. There's still something we don't agree on, though."

"What?"

"I still think your whole meaning of love is different from mine."

She suddenly felt like she was hitting a brick wall again. "Shall we go on, Aaron?" she asked patiently, hoping God would lead them to a Scripture that would clarify the meaning of agape love.

"No, not right now. Let me digest what we just read first."

"OK."

"Maybe it will sink in, sooner or later," he said. He brought her hand to his lips and kissed it tenderly. "Thank you for helping me."

"I've just been an instrument of the Lord."

He smiled. "Well, I thank Him, then!" He turned her hand over and kissed her palm, then each fingertip gently. Something stirred inside her. "Relax, Beth."

"I—I am relaxed."

"No you're not. You're all tense."

Her throat went dry when he drew her close to him, and she stiffened. "See?" he said. "Tense." She didn't answer. "Let's just sit like this awhile."

"Yes. It's nice."

She leaned her head on his shoulder and felt his lips brush against her hair. For a long time they sat like that. Bethany felt completely relaxed in the tranquility of the moment.

Then, suddenly, he cupped her chin with one hand and she saw passion smoldering in his eyes.

"Sweetheart," he whispered against her mouth. His lips crushed against hers with a force over which she had no control.

The apprehension she experienced over his sudden move outweighed the pleasure, and she tensed. Her hands were pinned against his chest and she could feel his heart beating swiftly.

"How long will they be gone?" he asked in a throaty whisper.

"They—a couple of hours, I guess, but—"

He kissed her again briefly, then with his lips still brushing against hers, said, "Beth, I want you so much."

As if an alarm suddenly went off somewhere inside her, she pulled loose from him and jumped to her feet. "No, Aaron! We've been through that!"

He stood up next to her and pressed her close to his body. "How can you kiss me like that and not want me?"

She pushed away from him. "Aaron, you don't understand. I *do* want you! But I just can't. I—I—Jesus means more to me than anything. Anyone."

His arms dropped to his sides, and for what seemed like an eternity he just stared at her and said nothing. Finally he spoke. "Beth, I'm not sure I'll try this again. It's just too frustrating."

"Aaron, I'm sorry."

"Yeah. Well, it's hard to believe that a warm-blooded woman like you can just turn it off like that."

She could feel tears rising in her throat. "Please try to understand."

"Uh-huh. Well, I'll try." He picked up his Bible and got his own coat from the closet, then headed for the door.

Tears brimmed on her lids. "Aaron?"

"I'll call you, Beth. I just have to think this out." And he left.

The tears spilled over. She felt alone, defeated. What started out to be such a glorious evening swiftly turned into heartbreak.

Wandering impotently to the kitchen, she looked at the cup of tea she had poured earlier. Suddenly, she didn't feel like a warm-blooded woman. She felt confused and unfulfilled and untouched. And about as cold as the tea in the little china cup that she had never tasted.

CHAPTER 8

FOR THE REST OF the week, Bethany spent as much time as possible with Calvin Bruce. She saw Aaron on the set but it was usually from a distance and the moment the shooting was over for the day she left. She knew he had to get out of his makeup and wardrobe and that always took time.

She just couldn't face him right now, after the conversation they had had. And certainly not after the manner in which Vivian Gordon had pasted herself to Aaron's side all week on the set.

Well, apparently there really *was* something serious to the relationship he had with Vivian. It was too bad, she lamented, because Aaron Steele needed someone to uplift him spiritually right now and Vivian Gordon certainly wasn't doing that. Yet, he was all man. And no doubt he had needs and was used to having those needs fulfilled. And since one Bethany Jordan wasn't going to give in to his desires, he had obviously found someone else who would. Bethany carried this somber thought around with her like a shroud until Nora confronted her with it on the next morning.

"Beth, something is surely troubling you, I can tell that. I don't mean to be nosy if you don't want to talk about it. But I'll pray with you if you want me to."

Bethany swallowed hard at the lump in her throat, still refusing to give in to tears. "Thanks, Nora. It's—it's Aaron."

"I figured it was. He called last night while you were out with Cal."

"He did?"

"Yes. I didn't leave a note because I wasn't sure you'd see it anyway. He sounded a little ticked."

She shrugged. "I can't help that. Anyway, I'm sure he's not lonesome."

"How do you know that?"

"Because he has Vivian!" The tears were now brimming on her lids, threatening to spill over, but she blinked them away.

"He works with Vivian, Bethany," Nora said gently.

"Hah! It's a little more than work, Nora!"

"Are you sure?"

"Yes! I overheard them talking on Monday. She was asking him if he wanted her to go to his house again that night!"

"So?"

"Nora!" she exasperated. "Besides, when he was here Tuesday we had another argument. I'm sure Vivian doesn't argue with him! Isn't it obvious?"

"Only one thing is obvious. We need to pray about this. I don't think you're being fair to Aaron, jumping to conclusions."

Looking at her friend through a blur of tears, it was

certain that she was going to cry. There was no holding back the burning tears now.

They held hands and prayed and Bethany could feel her spirits lifting as they prayed, as though some heavy burden was being removed from her shoulders. When they finished, they hugged each other affectionately.

"Now then," Nora said, "everything is going to be fine. I just know it."

Bethany nodded, still struggling to bring her tears under control.

"Besides," Nora continued, "look what just happened outside!"

Bethany turned to look out the window. The rain had stopped. The sky was cloudless.

And the sun was shining.

When Nora announced later on in the afternoon, that Aaron was on the phone, Bethany was at first tempted not to talk to him. But after Nora's somewhat impatient gestures and grimaces coupled with an unmistakably Divine shove, she picked up the receiver.

"Aaron?"

"Well! Don't tell me you're home! I suppose you're rushing around, getting ready to go out with Cal?"

His sarcasm annoyed her, and she swallowed back an angry reply. "No, as a matter of fact, I wasn't. Nora and I were just talking."

"Are you busy tonight?"

"I don't have plans, other than my work, if that's what you mean. I'm always busy with that."

"Ah, yes! And I'm sure Cal is doing a good job of keeping you occupied when you aren't writing!"

Oh, dear God! The anger in his voice! How was she to cope with it?

"Aaron, I told you before, more than once actually, that it is nothing but business between me and Cal. This past week he's been kind enough to take me to dinner a few times, but we still talked about my writing. He's my agent, if you will recall. He's interested in my talent as a writer. The more successful I am, the more money he makes. That may sound a little mercenary, but those are the facts, nonetheless." She took a deep breath. "And I appreciated his company this past week, especially since I hadn't heard from you," she added.

Aaron was silent a moment. When he spoke again, his voice had softened considerably. "Yes. Well, I'm sorry. I have been busy."

Her mind flashed with Vivian Gordon. "I'm sure you have."

"Anyway, I did try to call you a couple of times but you were out with Cal."

"Yes."

"And I never could seem to catch up with you on the set. Every time I finished for the day, you had already left."

"Yes, I guess that's true." She remembered how she had hurried out after the day's shooting, just to avoid a confrontation with him. She probably should have stayed and at least heard what he had to say. That would have been the fair thing to do.

"Well, what about tonight?" he asked impatiently.

"What did you have in mind?"

"Dinner?"

"Yes. Fine, Aaron. I'd—I'd enjoy that."

"Me too," he said softly. "I'll pick you up at seven."

Nora came into the room just as Bethany hung up the phone. "Is it the absence of rain outside that's making you so bubbly?" she asked with a grin.

Bethany smiled. "Well, of course the bright sunshine after such awful weather *does* do wonders for the spirit, Nora!" she replied. "But a date with Aaron Steele does a lot for the morale, too!"

Nora gave her a hug. "I'm so glad," she said. "You two are awfully good together!"

Bethany couldn't help but agree, even though she still had apprehensions. There was the ominous cloud of Vivian Gordon, for one thing, that hovered over their relationship. But it was Aaron's stubborn refusal to become a believer and see the true meaning of love that bothered her most of all.

Aaron never seemed to disappoint her insofar as his looks were concerned. He was splendid in a sport coat of burgundy wool, gray slacks, and a shirt that was a lighter shade of gray. Bethany stifled an impulse to throw her arms around him and kiss him.

He looked at her with admiration. The sheer wool ivory-colored dress she had chosen to wear was undoubtedly a good choice, judging from his expression. His eyes traveled over her slim figure then back to gaze into her own, and she shivered with excitement.

"You look beautiful!" he said.

"Thank you," she replied in a whisper. "I'll—I'll get my coat."

Nora came out of the kitchen with a Cheshire cat grin. She held a package in her hands. "Are you two, by any chance, going near Santa Monica?"

"As a matter of fact, we're going to have dinner

near there," he said. "Is there something we can do for you, Nora?"

"If you could, I'd appreciate it so much! I have a friend who has a home by the sea, and her front porch was badly damaged by the storm. She lives alone and hasn't much money and I baked her some bread. I called her a while ago, and she said she would be home this evening."

"Sure, we can go by her place."

"Oh, wonderful! Her name is Judy Richards, and here's where she lives." She handed Aaron a slip of paper.

He read the address. "Right. I know just where that is," he said. "You say you called her—did you—er, say who would be coming by with the bread?"

Nora smiled. "I just told her Aaron and Beth. It doesn't matter. She won't pester you for an autograph."

He laughed. "You're sure about that?"

"I'm sure. She's blind."

They decided to see Judy Richards first. She lived in an unpretentious little house, very much secluded from other surrounding homes by trees and shrubbery. It was also a distance from neighboring houses, and Bethany wondered if that was wise for a handicapped person, especially since Nora had said Judy lived alone. But she wasn't alone, they realized. When they drove down a steep driveway to the front of the house, they could hear a dog barking.

Bethany had a feeling something was wrong, and she clutched at Aaron's arm as they neared the front of the house. Her fears were justified.

As they made their way through some thick, juniper

bushes the little front porch came into view. Broken pillars had been replaced by solid two by fours, undoubtedly awaiting proper repair and finishing. Crouched low on the wooden porch floor was a young, very thin woman.

Her straight, dark blonde hair was tied with a blue ribbon, and she wore a darker blue cotton dress with a full shirt. Her face was plain but rather pretty. As they got closer to her they could see she was wincing in pain. The large, German Shepherd dog sitting next to her stopped barking, bared his teeth, and uttered a low growl.

"Quiet, Melvin," the woman said. "Who's there, please?" Sightless, pale blue eyes strained to see in vain.

"It's OK, Judy," Aaron said. "We're Aaron and Beth. Nora said we were coming."

"Oh, yes! Oh!" In an attempt to get up, she only cried out in agony.

"What's wrong?" Bethany exclaimed. She took one step closer then backed up as the dog growled again, showing his strong white teeth as another threat.

"Melvin, it's OK," Judy said. "They're friends. *Friends!*" She reached out to pat the dog on the head, and he whimpered softly and settled down beside her.

Apparently the dog was not convinced the visitors would do not harm to his beloved mistress. Still, he stayed close to her side.

They approached cautiously. The young woman's foot was caught between some broken boards and bleeding badly. She waved a careless hand, trying to appear brave, and managed a brief smile, but her face soon contorted in pain again.

"It was stupid of me," she said. "I knew this part of the porch wasn't fixed yet. They're supposed to take care of it Monday. But I thought I heard a car, and I came outside and forgot—oh! Oh, it hurts!" Tears filled Judy's eyes, and Bethany reached for her hand.

"You'll be OK, Judy. Can you lift your foot out of there?"

"N—no, I don't think . . ."

"She's twisted her ankle badly," Aaron said. "And there's a nasty cut that's bleeding pretty hard. I'd like to have a doctor check this, if it's OK with you, Judy."

"Oh, well—yes, I suppose it would be best."

Aaron knelt down on the porch and pulled at the broken boards, being careful not to injure Judy further, until he had worked loose the ones around her trapped foot. Then he gently lifted the slight young woman in his arms and headed for the car. "Come on," he said. "You too, Melvin." The dog obediently followed. "There's an emergency hospital not far from here."

Several people turned to look as they went into the emergency entrance of the hospital. One nurse stopped him with, "Oh! Aren't you . . ." But he brought a warning finger to his lips, for her to be quiet. Once Judy was in the examining room Aaron went to the desk and asked that Judy's bills be sent to him.

"That was generous of you," Bethany said as they walked over to a vending machine for a cup of coffee.

He merely waved his hand impatiently. "Better take cream in this stuff," he said, pushing the proper buttons. "It's really terrible coffee. Always is in these vending machines."

They sat in silence, sipping the truly terrible coffee, and waited. Bethany silently prayed for the young blind woman. How sad not to be able to see, she thought. How fortunate people were that could see, and how it seemed to be taken for granted, to have sight. It was another blessing to count, she reflected.

At length, Judy was brought out in a wheel chair. Her seeing-eye dog had been permitted to go into the examining room with her, but the nurse said some hospitals did not permit it. They had personally found that it was easier to let the dog remain by the master's side as long as there was ample room in the examining room, since some dogs became too nervous if they had to remain outside in the waiting room.

Judy was smiling. While a nurse showed her the proper use of crutches, the doctor came over to where Bethany and Aaron were sitting. They both stood up anxiously.

"Are you relatives of Miss Richards?" the doctor asked.

"No, just friends," Bethany answered.

"I see. Well, she's sprained her ankle and cut up her foot pretty badly. Nothing is broken, though. Did she say she lives alone?"

Aaron spoke up. "With her dog, yes."

The doctor rubbed his chin. "Amazing how those blind people get along like that," he said. "They know where everything is. Seem to be wonderfully self-sufficient!"

"Yes, that's quite true," Aaron agreed.

"Except that now she'll have to use crutches for a while. I think she should have some help during the day."

"I believe that can easily be arranged," Aaron said.

"I know Nora will want to go see her," Bethany added. "And I could, too. Or did you think a nurse should be there, doctor?"

"There's probably no need for a nurse," he said, "as long as she has caring friends like you." He smiled at them. "I've given her a prescription for pain. You can get it filled in the pharmacy. I'll need to see her in a week."

Aaron shook his head. "Thank you, doctor. I'm glad she's going to be OK."

"She'll be fine." He studied Aaron a minute, then grinned. "Did anyone ever tell you that you're a dead ringer for Aaron Steele?"

While Aaron was getting the prescription filled, Bethany called Nora and told her what had happened.

Nora was shocked. "Is the doctor certain there's nothing broken?" she asked.

"He's positive. She'll be fine."

"Does she have to go back to the hospital?"

"The doctor wants to see her in a week. I guess it would be in his office."

"Oh. Is she in pain?"

"Yes, a little. But there's a prescription that should take care of that."

"I'll leave as soon as I get a sitter for Timmy. Can you stay with her until I get there?"

"Sure. Only you don't have to—"

"Beth, I want to. Sure you can stay?"

"Yes. We'd be happy to. We'll take her home now."

"Don't you have to ask Aaron?"

"No. He'll agree."

108

Bethany knew that Aaron would be agreeable to staying with Judy until Nora arrived. She had seen something in Aaron Steele tonight that she hadn't seen before. She had seen him display compassion and kindness and help to another human being who was in need, without a single thought to himself. What he did tonight was pleasing to God.

As soon as they were inside Judy's little house and had made the young woman fairly comfortable, Judy expressed her gratitude.

"I just don't know how to thank you," she said. "You two have been so kind."

"Heavens Judy! We simply did what anyone would have done," Bethany replied.

"No, not anyone. Hardly anyone." Judy smiled. "You two must be Christians!"

Aaron opened his mouth but Bethany quickly spoke up first. "Are you a believer, Judy?"

"Oh, yes! And I'm so glad I am!"

"I know the feeling!"

Judy turned to where she knew Aaron was sitting. "And you, Aaron. You're such a kind man. So full of compassion. Of Christian love."

Aaron looked at Bethany enigmatically. In his eyes she read confusion. A thousand questions. "Christian love?" he seemed to be asking her. "Me?"

They left Judy soon after Nora arrived. As he drove up the hill to the highway, Bethany noticed a self-satisfied smile playing on his lips.

"I'll bet you're starved!" he said.

She laughed. "Now that you mention it."

"Do you think I got all the splinters out of my pants?"

"I think so. You look fine."

"Sure?"

"Yes." Beautiful, she wanted to add. Glowing, radiant, alive—all of the adjectives that properly describe the countenance of one who has just served the Lord.

"Well, you still look as lovely as you did when I first picked you up," he said.

"I should still look presentable. I didn't pull a porch apart with my bare hands!"

He shrugged. "Do you like Greek food?" he asked, changing the subject.

"I don't think I've ever had any."

"No? Well, you're in for a treat!"

Bethany had to agree in the delicious taste of the food. Their dinner began with appetizers of Greek olives, Feta cheese, and what the waitress called Toursi, which were simply pickled vegetables. Bethany could have made a meal out of just the appetizers, but there was, of course, much more.

The main course was Greek roast lamb, with rice pilaf, artichokes, and a delicious salad with chunks of crisp lettuce, slivered green peppers and scallions and other fresh vegetables. The salad was tossed with a dressing of olive oil and vinegar and a dash of oregano. They were served a Greek bread with a thick crust and for dessert, Baklava, delicious layers of thin sheets of pastry and nut filling, drenched with some kind of syrup.

When they finished, Bethany sighed. "My goodness! I don't know if I can walk out of here, I ate so much!"

He laughed. "Me, too! But I still have room for one more cup of coffee. How about you?"

"Maybe half a cup."

The waitress refilled their cups and they both sipped the hot beverage thoughtfully.

"It's been quite an evening, hasn't it, Beth?"

"Yes."

"I like Judy. She's a sweet little lady."

"She certainly is."

"We'll have to go back and visit her sometime."

"I'd like that. And I'm sure she would."

"That's a really good dog she has, too."

"Yes, he's special, all right," she said in agreement. "Aaron, you were very dear tonight."

"Dear? Come on, Beth!"

"Now don't sell yourself so short!"

"Anyone would have done what I did, Beth!"

"I don't think so. You acted tonight just like Jesus would have acted."

"Oh, come on! Are you going to start that again?"

"Why do you fight it so, Aaron? You heard Judy. She said you acted in Christian love!"

He stared at her silently, his eyes full of confusion again.

"In the play, Aaron, you will say the words as the Apostle John: 'This is love, my children! Not just words and talk but true love, which shows itself in action.' Have you been studying those lines?"

"Of course I have!"

"Then tonight should have helped you, Aaron! You gave of yourself tonight, unselfishly. You showed Christian love to a complete stranger."

Again, he looked at her in puzzlement. "That's not the way Vivian interpreted that passage."

"Vivian?"

"Yes. She's been coming over to my place almost every night."

Bethany was shocked that he would admit it so openly and without any signs of embarrassment! She pushed her coffee cup away from her. "I—think we'd better go, if you're finished, Aaron."

He frowned. "Fine. Sure. Whatever you say."

He headed back away from the beach and Bethany was a little disappointed that he wasn't going to drive to their favorite spot by the sea for a while. But she said nothing. Perhaps he was overly tired, she thought, from all the activity of the evening.

They drove the freeway in silence. Bethany's thoughts were muddled over the fact that he could be so kind and compassionate one minute and openly brazen the next about his affair with Vivian. She turned from him and stared out the window so he wouldn't notice her confused expression and interrogate her.

Suddenly, she saw a car on the shoulder of the freeway, and an elderly man attempting to change a tire. She started to say something but Aaron had already driven by the parked car.

"Did you see that?" he asked.

"That old man back there?"

"Yes! Trying to change a tire! He looked like he was one hundred years old!"

"He did look old, but I didn't get a very good look."

"Neither did I. That's what I'm going to do." He turned off at the next exit and in minutes was back on the freeway, approaching the spot where they had seen the parked car.

The old man was still there, still struggling with the tire, while other motorists raced by, ignoring him completely.

Aaron pulled to a stop just ahead of the man, and when they got out Bethany was startled to find out the man was quite a bit older than she had thought.

"Hi, there!" Aaron called. "Need some help?"

The old man squinted up at Aaron over his bifocals. "You bet! Can you really help me, young fella?"

"I'll give it a good try! Is that the spare?"

"Yep," he said, straightening up. " 'Fraid the other tire's shot. I only hope this spare is OK. I don't have much farther to go to get home." He looked at Bethany. "Went to see my sister tonight. She fixed me meat loaf. Fixes it real good, that one. Puts cracker crumbs in it, just the way I like it. She's a widow, and I lost my wife two years ago so it's good we have each other."

Bethany smiled. "It certainly is."

"She's older than me," he said with a chuckle. "Not too many people are!" He bent over to inspect Aaron's work. "What do you think?" he asked.

"The spare looks OK. I'll get it on and then we'll be able to tell."

The old man smiled at Bethany. "Pretty little missis you have here," he said. Before Aaron or Bethany could say anything to the contrary, he went on. "Kinda nice to see such a natural looking beauty these days. She could be a movie star! You a movie star?" he asked Bethany.

She laughed and shook her head. "No! Hardly!"

"Oh, you could be!" the old man insisted. "Now take your husband here. He's a nice looking young fella too, but he couldn't be a movie star, 'cause there's too many nice looking fellas like that, you see. But there aren't many like you, young lady!"

Bethany suppressed a giggle. "Well, thank you."

He rambled on while Aaron worked on the tire. "Not too many folks willin' to stop and help out these days," he said. "Used to be that people would stop and offer a hand all the time but not now. Folks are too afraid, I guess. Too many nuts running around."

Aaron finally stood up and rubbed at his back. "There you go," he said. "Looks like she'll get you there!"

"Well now, that's great. What do I owe you, young man?"

"Oh, please! Nothing!"

The old man shook his head as he fished in a pocket and pulled out a well-worn leather coin purse. "Nope! I insist! Now, I'm a proud man and I don't take charity." He opened the purse and shook some change out into the palm of his other hand, then extended the money to Aaron. "Here now, you did a good job. Figure that'd be worth about fifty cents! Buy something for the missis!"

Aaron took the money and nodded. "Well, thank you, but—"

The old man raised his hand to silence him. "Think nothing of it!" he said. "Much obliged!" And he got into the old car and drove off.

Bethany glowed with love and admiration for Aaron. "That was dear of you to do that," she said as they got into the car.

"There you go again! What's 'dear' about helping an old man like that? He was so frail a strong wind would have blown him right off the freeway! Besides, Beth," he said with a grin, "I made us fifty cents, didn't I?"

She laughed. "I'm glad you took it. He would have been hurt if you refused his money."

"I could see that. He's of a proud generation."

"Well anyway, you did it again!" she said with a smile.

"What?"

"You acted in Christian love!"

"Oh, Beth!" he exasperated.

"Didn't you ever hear the story of the good Samaritan?" she asked.

"Sure, I did. In Sunday School. A man was lying by the side of the road, all beaten up, and everyone passed by him. Finally a Samaritan came by and took care of him."

"Yes. Jesus said when you do kind things for others it's the same as doing it for Him!"

Aaron stared straight ahead and didn't answer her as he drove.

"You know, I believe God placed those people in your path tonight, Aaron. First Judy, then the old man. And you certainly didn't disappoint Him."

"Come on." He looked embarrassed.

He pulled up in front of the house and turned off the ignition. "Let's change the subject," he said. "I need to ask you a question."

"Certainly. Anything."

"What's this thing you have against Vivian?"

Bethany stiffened. "I—I don't know what you mean, Aaron."

"Stop lying. Christians aren't supposed to tell lies, are they?"

She shook her head. "No."

"Well, then?"

She opened the car door. "I'd better get in," she said.

He sighed and got out of the car. As he walked around the other side he jumped. "What was that?"

"What was what?"

"Oh, no! Look!" He pointed inside the car.

Bethany bent down and peered inside and saw a big white cat with one black ear on the front seat. "Where'd that come from?" she asked.

"Beats me," he said. "It came out of nowhere! I felt something brush against my legs and it startled me." He stared at the cat and shook his head. "I never saw a cat jump into a car before," he said. "I didn't think they liked to ride."

"Most cats don't."

"Does it belong to someone around here?"

"I don't think so. It probably needs a home."

"Don't look at me!"

"Aaron, my mother has a theory about cats jumping into strange cars."

"What's that?"

"Well, it happens so seldom that my mother believes when a cat does that, it belongs to you!"

He laughed. "Are you serious?"

"Yes."

"You just made that up!"

"No, honest! That's what my mother thinks!"

"What would I do with a cat?"

"Care for it. Love it."

"Come on, Beth."

"It needs a home, Aaron."

"Not my home."

"It needs love."

"Not my love."

"It's one of God's creatures. Maybe the Lord caused it to cross your path to see what you would do. Just like Judy and the old man."

He stared at her a moment, frowning. Then he

shrugged and closed the car door. "Well, since I have splinters and car grease on my clothes now, I guess a little cat hair won't matter. Besides, I can always take it to the pound in the morning."

She smiled up at him. "But you won't!"

"Don't look at me like that," he said. "I'm hard as nails about cats."

"Sure you are. I can tell!"

"Come on, I'll walk you to the door."

They stood by the door a minute. "How about fixing me a cup of coffee?"

"Oh, gee, I don't know. I mean, everyone's sleeping."

"I'll be quiet."

"Well ..."

"Instant is OK."

"All right."

He followed her into the kitchen. "Let's get back to the subject of Vivian," he said. "You were going to tell me what you have against her."

"I was?"

"Yes, you were."

She put the water on to boil. "Vivian is—well, she just doesn't seem right for you, Aaron."

"No? Who is, then?"

Her heart pounded. "I—I don't know. But Vivian is so—"

"Attractive? Sexy? Willing? She's all of the above. You have to admit that."

"Y–yes."

"Now you, for example. You are very attractive. Much more than Vivian, as far as I'm concerned."

"Oh, please!" She knew her looks couldn't be compared with the flawless beauty of Vivian Gordon.

"Yes, you are! And sexy. You're very sexy." He came over to her and one of his fingers traveled slowly down her arm.

The spoon rattled against the side of the mug as she measured the coffee. She swallowed hard. "I would hardly call myself sexy," she said in a hoarse whisper.

"Oh, yes," he said, pulling her close to him. "I'm a very good judge of what is sexy in a woman," he said.

"Oh, Aaron! Really! I . . ." But her words were unfinished. He tilted her chin upward and kissed her long and hard. For a while she yielded to his passionate kissing until little warning signals flashed in her mind and she began to stiffen.

He let loose of her abruptly. "Yes, you are beautiful and you are sexy. But willing you are not!"

Bethany felt a lump in her throat. "And Vivian is."

"Exactly."

"I—I see." Her hands still trembled as she poured the water over the coffee. "Do you—do you want your coffee in here or in the living room?" she asked.

"I'd rather have you than coffee."

"Let's—let's go into the living room. I—I think it will be quieter," she said in a squeeky voice.

He followed her in. "Why do you have to fight me so much?" he asked.

She placed the mugs on the table. "I'm not fighting you. I'm fighting sin."

He pulled her into his arms again. "How can anything so beautiful be sinful? Explain that!"

"Aaron, we've been over this so much! Remember last Tuesday when we studied about being in the world?"

"I don't want a trip through space right now, thank you. You know what I want!"

118

She pushed away from him. "Yes! I know what you want! And it has *nothing* to do with love!" She could feel the incriminating tears pushing at her eyes again.

"What are you talking about? If physical love isn't—"

"*See?*" she interrupted hotly. "That's all you are thinking about!"

He stared at her in anger. "Just like I said, willing you are not!"

"Well, there's always Vivian!"

"You bet!"

"And—is she going to continue to come over to your house like she had been this past week?"

"I suppose she will. She's willing. I told you that. And Vivian isn't afraid of what people will think by coming to my house."

Bethany bit her lip to still its trembling. "Maybe—maybe you'd better go, Aaron."

He glared at her. "Maybe I'd better!" He opened the door then faced her again. "And if Vivian isn't available at least I'll have a cat to keep me warm tonight!"

CHAPTER 9

JESUS WEPT.

Bethany wondered how many Christians clung to that Scripture at times in their own lives when sadness and weeping seemed endless.

Because her eyes were still swollen from crying herself to sleep the night before, she wore sun glasses to church Sunday morning. Neither Nora nor Frank commented on it, although she noticed a few sympathetic glances from both of them from time to time. She knew her attitude was wrong and would have to be put right before the day was out.

As soon as they got back to the house, Bethany excused herself and withdrew to her room to write. At least that was her intention. But the words wouldn't come. She sat at her typewriter and stared at the blank sheet of paper until the tears rolled down her cheeks again. She could only think of Aaron. Aaron and Vivian.

Why had he injected Vivian into their conversation?

And what possible "interpretation" could Vivian have given to those precious lines of Christian love? Why in the world would he be discussing the meaning of the lines with Vivian anyway? Surely the time they were spending together was not spent in Christian love. Hardly. It was more like the meaning Aaron gave to love. Physical love. Lust.

A sense of shame washed over her as the Scripture came to her mind, ". . . forgiving one another, even as God, for Christ's sake, hath forgiven you."

She recalled a time when she was a little girl and accidentally let the screen door slam shut on the tail of Maggie, the family cat. Maggie let out one ferocious yell, gave Bethany a look that would cause frost to form on a wood-burning stove, and ran from the room. It was a long time before the cat would let Bethany come near her, so unforgiving was the cat's spirit toward the person who had done her such injury.

Now Bethany was dangerously close to acting like that cat. Aaron had hurt her. He may not be aware of it right now, but if she continued to harbor an unforgiving spirit, he would see it soon enough. And the barrier that she was permitting to rise between her and Aaron, would not only widen, it would also disrupt her fellowship with God.

She stood and paced around the room. She had to clear her mind of these intruding, depressing thoughts once and for all, or she would never have the peace of mind that God intended her to have. She was dwelling on things she had no business fretting about.

She sat down and prayed, confessing her feelings for Aaron to God—releasing to Him all the emotions that were causing her such anguish. She gave it all to

God and when she finished, she was once more filled with peace.

Taking a deep breath, she left her room to find Nora and Frank and share her feelings with them. They were in the living room, talking to Timmy and motioned her to sit down while they finished. Was it all right, he needed to know, for him to pray about a bird he had seen outside his window that was having trouble flying.

"Timmy," his father began, "that little bird must be important to you, so of course it's OK to pray about it."

"God won't mind?"

"Certainly not! God cares about that little bird, too."

"He does?"

"You bet He does!"

"That little bird was just lying on the grass. Will God make the bird all better again so he can fly?"

Frank hesitated a moment and Bethany could tell that he was struggling for the right answer. "Timmy, I'll tell you something," he said. "God can do anything."

"OK, dad. Thanks!" He started to leave the room, then turned. "Oh—there's something else."

"What's that?" Frank asked.

"Well, remember the people that lived down the street? They were here from Phila—Phila. . . ."

"Philadelphia," Nora said patiently.

"Yeah! Well anyway, they moved away again."

"So soon? They were only here about a month!"

"I know."

Nora and Frank exchanged questioning glances, trying to figure out what that had to do with the injured bird.

"They left their big white cat," Timmy said.

"They *left* it?" Frank exclaimed.

"Yeah. But if the cat gets hungry, won't it eat that bird?"

"Wait a minute," Bethany said. "Did you say it was a big white cat?"

"Yes. Will he eat that bird?"

"Did the cat have one black ear?"

"Yeah! Did you see him?"

"I certainly did. Last night."

The little boy looked worried. "But the bird—"

"Not to worry," Bethany said reassuringly. "Aaron took the cat home."

"Aaron?" Nora exclaimed.

Bethany smiled. "Yes. It jumped in his car."

Frank looked surprised. "I've never heard of a cat doing that before."

"It doesn't happen very often. My mother said if a cat does that, then the owner of the car had better keep it."

"Well, I guess Aaron has a cat, then." Nora said.

"You mean I don't have to worry about that cat eating the bird, Dad?"

"No, son. I guess not. You can go and pray for the little bird now. And Timmy?"

"Yes, Dad?"

"Nothing is too big for God's power and nothing is too small for His love. Remember that."

"OK, Dad, I will." He ran from the room.

Frank took a deep breath. "Oh, boy," he said with a grin. "Sometimes it's hard to know what to say. But I believe the boy has enough faith."

Bethany was impressed. "I think I just learned a lot about child-raising," she said.

123

Nora gave her husband an affectionate pat on the arm. "Some people don't agree with us, in that we encourage Timmy to pray for things he considers important," she said. "But we feel that his priorities will change as he gets older and things of importance will be much different as time goes on."

"The most vital thing," Frank said, "is that we encourage him to pray at any time. Not just at bedtime or before meals, but we pray when feelings are hurt or when there's a need for guidance or a reason to praise God. We pray without ceasing, in other words."

"I think that's beautiful," Bethany replied. "I hope I'm as good with my own children some day."

Nora smiled. "I'm sure you will be. By the way, are you feeling better?"

"Yes, thanks. I just wanted you two to know that I'm on the right track again," she said with a grin.

Frank leaned forward in his chair, hands clasped between his knees. "That right? Get it all ironed out with the Lord?"

"Yes."

"Frank and I kind of thought that's what you were doing!" Nora said.

"I prayed as David did. That God would renew a right spirit within me. I just gave it all to the Lord. All the frustration I've been feeling about Aaron and my own feelings about him. Everything."

"That's good," Frank said. "Now you have to leave it there. It's human nature to give something to God only to take it all back again!"

"I know! I've done that!"

"What about Aaron?" Nora asked. "Do you think he's getting any closer to believing?"

Bethany sighed. "I don't know, Nora. Sometimes—like last night. All the things he did were precious. So unselfish! Yet, when I told him so, he just talked about other things. He displays so much tenderness at times only he seems unable to deal with it. He just changes the subject."

"I think I know one of the reasons for that," Frank said. "His image, as far as the public is concerned, isn't exactly tenderness. Maybe he doesn't want to give up on that."

"I don't agree," Nora replied. "From a woman's standpoint, all heros should have a tender side to them, no matter how tough they appear."

"I believe Nora's right," Bethany said. "I think he's just embarrassed. Doesn't want anyone to think there's a soft spot under that muscled exterior."

Nora laughed. "Well, muscled he is, all right!"

"You should have seen him ripping up the boards around Judy's foot!"

"I'll bet that was a sight!" Nora said, still chuckling. "Oh, and speaking of Judy, I want to take a run out there this afternoon. Want to go with me, Beth?"

"Yes! I'd love to see how she's doing!"

"Would you mind staying here and looking after Timmy, Frank?"

"No, that's fine with me. I have some work to do in the garage anyway. Timmy can help me." He looked thoughtfully a moment. "Maybe I should bring that bird inside and see if I can tell what's wrong with it," he said.

Just as he said this, Timmy ran back into the room excitedly. "Guess what!" he cried. "I prayed that God would heal that little bird and He did! I watched it flap its wings and fly off, good as new!"

Bethany could only feel joy tugging at her heart. How much faith! How pleased the Lord must be with this little child! What a pity grown-ups couldn't possess such precious trust!

She looked at Timmy's eyes, wide with innocence, shining with happiness. A tear rolled down her cheek. Jesus expressed it best of all, she thought: ". . . of such is the kingdom of God."

It was a refreshing experience to visit with Judy again. Bethany had to marvel at the woman's ability to adapt to the use of crutches in spite of her blindness, although obviously, one of the blessings in Judy's life was Melvin. The dog seemed to sense that she was handicapped in more ways than one and walked ahead of her everywhere, whimpering softly as a warning if it looked like his mistress was about to bump into something with one of her crutches.

Judy was in excellent spirits and seemed to be getting on quite well. Almost immediately, she asked about Aaron.

"You two are very much in love, aren't you Beth?"

"Wha—oh, well—"

Judy laughed. "Oh, I don't mean to embarrass you! I could feel it though, you know. The love between you both. He really adores you, I could sense that. Are you getting married soon?"

"Uh—well, we—uh . . ."

"Oh, there I go again!" Judy said with a grin. "I'll never learn! You probably haven't agreed on a date yet and here I am, badgering you about it! But please invite me to the wedding, won't you, Beth?"

"Uh, yes—well . . ."

Nora spoke up quickly, and rescued Bethany from

her stammering. "You're right about those two. They *are* in love!"

"What does Aaron do?" Judy asked.

"Uh—well—he—uh—he's an actor," Bethany replied.

"Really? How exciting! Is he good?"

"I think so!"

"His public thinks so, too," Nora said. "You may as well know, Judy. His last name is Steele."

It took a moment for the news to sink in. "Aaron Steele?" Judy said in a whisper.

"Yes."

"Oh, my goodness! Well, I've never seen him, of course, but I've heard of him. A Hollywood reporter on the radio last week said he was going to do a religious play. Is that right?"

"Yes, it is," Nora replied.

"What's the name of it?"

" 'Agape, John.' Aaron will play the lead—the Apostle John."

Judy's face brightened. "How exciting! Is it a good play, do you think?"

Nora turned to Bethany and smiled. "Is it a good play, Beth?"

"I hope so!"

"Bethany wrote the play, Judy."

"Really? Honest? You mean I had two famous people in my home last night and I didn't even know it?"

Bethany laughed. "I can hardly be called famous! Not yet, anyway!"

"Well, if Aaron Steele is going to act in your play, you will be!"

They all laughed, then Judy became serious again. "I write a little too," she said modestly.

"You do? What do you write?" Bethany asked.

Judy lifted her slender shoulders in a shrug. She seemed embarrassed. "Poetry, mostly."

"Could I see some?"

"No, not yet. I mean, it needs work. Do you understand, Beth?"

"You bet I do!"

"I'll let you see it when I'm finished, though. I'm working on a book of poems. I use a tape recorder, then have someone type it for me."

"That sounds wonderful. I'll look forward to reading them when you've finished."

"And I'll look forward to hearing your play! My radio picks up the audio portion of certain TV channels, so I listen to a lot of TV! That probably sounds dumb, but I'm usually able to know what's going on by certain sounds."

"I don't think it's dumb," Bethany said. "I think it's wonderful!"

"Let me know when the play airs, OK?"

"I certainly will."

"And don't forget—when you and Aaron get married . . ."

"She'll invite you to the wedding, Judy. That's a promise, isn't it, Beth?"

"Well—uh—yes! Yes, of course!"

Bethany was somewhat relieved when they left. Not that it wasn't good to see Judy again and talk with her about her interest in poetry, but the discussion of her and Aaron was unnerving. She was a trifle piqued at Nora for joining in and feeding the subject, until Nora commented about it on the way home.

"Beth, you have to realize that sometimes when a

person loses one of the senses, others become stronger. Judy only brought out what I've been suspecting all along. Aaron is in love with you."

"Oh, Nora!"

"Believe it. And it will all come out in time. You gave it to God. Let Him work it out!"

"I know. But Aaron's not a Christian yet, Nora."

"You have to trust the Lord for that. You do love Aaron, don't you?"

"Does it show that much?"

"It sure does!"

Bethany laughed and relaxed a little. She had to remember, God was in charge. She had to "stand still." And wait.

The Bible study group was at the McKenzie house Tuesday night because the people that were supposed to have it had an outbreak of chicken pox in their household.

All evening Bethany kept hoping Aaron might show up but he didn't. She wondered also, if she should have phoned him and asked him to come. As the evening progressed, she was convinced she should have done just that. She should have put aside her personal hurt and humbled herself into calling him.

Glenn Davidson communicated with her from time to time with looks of understanding. He seemed to know what was bothering her and his eyes said perceptively, "It's OK, Beth. God understands."

His empathy made her feel considerably better but she still had regrets over not calling Aaron.

They studied from Psalm 25 and when they came to verse 8, Frank read it. "Good and upright is the Lord; therefore He instructs sinners in His ways."

A lengthy discussion followed on the importance of witnessing to nonbelievers and instructing new believers in the Word of God.

Bethany thought of Aaron and again felt remorse over not being more persistent in her witness to him.

But again, Glenn caught her attention and seemed to be reading her mind. When he spoke he addressed the whole group, but Bethany knew he was speaking primarily to her.

"We shouldn't be discouraged, though, over things," he said. "One of the main problems, I believe, that brings discouragement to a Christian is to get no immediate response when witnessing to a nonbeliever." He pointed to his open Bible. "Read ahead a little," he said, "to Psalm 27. Look at what verse 14 says." Then he read it out loud. "Wait on the Lord; be of good courage, and He shall strengthen thine heart. . . ." He paused and looked at Bethany as he finished read the verse: ". . . wait, I say, on the Lord."

The next day, the crew and part of the cast of "Agape John" went on location to a quiet and private beach where they could shoot a few exterior scenes of the fishermen spreading their nets on the sand, and of Jesus teaching by the seaside.

She and Calvin got their lunch from the catering truck that was parked nearly and they were sitting on a blanket that was spread over the sand. Bethany was glad she had worn her warm buckskin jacket since the wind was chilling.

"How are you doing on the next play, Beth?" he asked.

She raised the collar of the jacket and fastened it closer to her neck. "OK, I guess."

"Just OK?"

"I get a little writer's block now and then."

He eyed her shrewdly. "That's common. If you're sure that's what it is."

"What do you mean?"

He shrugged and took a bite of his sandwich. "Just wondered if anything else was bothering you," he said. "Of course, with you Christians, it's hard to tell."

"It is?"

"Sure is. Your world may be falling apart and you're still smiling," he said with a grin.

"Oh, not always!" She looked out to the shoreline, where Aaron was standing and talking to the director.

"It seems that way. How are you and Aaron doing?"

She jerked her head around to meet his questioning look. "What do you mean?"

"Just wondered how you and mighty man of Steele—pardon the pun—are getting along. Been out with him lately?"

"Uh—Saturday. Last Saturday."

He sighed. "Better watch it, honey. I told you before, I don't want you hurt. It's pretty obvious you've fallen for him."

She bristled a little. Did the whole world know she was in love with Aaron Steele? "Cal, really, I—"

"Now don't say it again, Beth."

"Don't say what again?"

"That you don't know what I mean." He washed the sandwich down with a sip of hot coffee. "Want to go out tonight? I can get tickets to a concert."

"Not tonight, Cal. Thanks, Anyway." She noticed Aaron was looking in her direction. He was shading his eyes from the sun, frowning.

"I'll take a raincheck, though!" she said with a smile.

Cal gave her a brief hug. "That's my girl!" he said.

Aaron was still watching them, she noticed, and still scowling.

Calvin carefully peeled an orange and separated it into sections. "Here," he said, handing her a segment. "Good for you. Lots of Vitamin C."

"Thanks! Um, it looks good!" She took a bite and the juice spurted out and ran down through her fingers.

He grabbed a napkin and handed it to her, then brought another one up to his face. "Right in the eye!" he said, laughing. "The juice went right in my eye!"

"Oh, no! Are you all right?"

He was still chuckling, blinking his eye comically. "Fine! Just fine! I always keep one eye shut like this!"

Bethany laughed with him. "It is a good orange, though!"

"Here, have another piece," he said. "Only this time, keep your Vitamin C to yourself!"

She laughed again, then noticed Aaron from a distance. He was casting furtive glances in her direction, shaking off the attempts of the makeup man to repair his makeup, and yelling at one of the crew members to adjust a reflector that was "nearly blinding him."

He was in a wretched mood, she noticed. How could he possibly impart the right amount of emotion to his lines in a mood like that? Was it because he was watching her and Calvin? Was he upset because she was laughing and enjoying herself?

She also noticed, though, that he wasn't the only one observing the seemingly intimate conversation between her and Calvin. To one side of them was a trailer. And inside the open doorway, Vivian Gordon was watching intently, a self-satisfied smirk curving on her mouth.

Bethany had always known that the first thing to do when anxious or distressed was to have a good talk with the Lord. She had heard once that when a Christian reaches up as far as he can, that God will reach down the rest of the way.

This wasn't easy where Vivian was concerned. There was something in the way she was looking at Bethany and Cal at the beach that was truly distressing. Vivian seemed to be reading something in the scene she had witnessed that just wasn't there. Furthermore, it seemed to please the actress in a distorted, illogical sort of way.

But Bethany said nothing to Frank and Nora about it when she returned. She simply committed it to prayer, as she had done with all the other ill feelings that had cropped up before.

When Aaron called at six o'clock, she thought at first it might be answered prayer, but after his initial remark, she wasn't so sure.

His voice reeked with sarcasm. "You and Cal sure had one whale of a good time today, didn't you?"

"Now, Aaron—"

"Now, Aaron!" he mocked in a whiny voice. "I saw him take you into his arms, Beth. Don't deny it!"

"Aaron! It was just a small hug. A friendly hug!"

"Sure it was!"

"It was!"

"It looked like a lot more than that from where I was standing!"

Bethany's heart was pounding. "It *wasn't* anything, Aaron!" she replied as calmly as possible. "Don't treat it like it meant something—because it didn't."

"Uh-huh."

"You were pretty far away, so I hardly think you're in a position to make such a decisive observation."

"I was far away."

"Yes, you were."

"But Vivian wasn't."

"What?"

"Vivian saw you from the trailer. She told me what was going on."

Bethany was getting more than irritated. So that was the cause of Vivian's feline expression! No doubt she couldn't wait to run to Aaron with a full account of what she saw. Or *thought* she saw. Or perhaps *wished* she had seen.

"Vivian saw nothing that was wrong," she said quietly.

"That's your story."

"Aaron!" she said with a sudden burst of anger. "Do you realize how childish you're being?"

"What's this sudden rage I'm hearing? Guilt?"

She stomped her foot and was glad he couldn't see it. "I have nothing to be guilty about, Aaron! Calvin is a dear friend and that's all!"

"Uh-huh. I suppose you and your dear friend are going out tonight?"

"He did ask me, but—"

"That's what I thought! No use my asking you out, then!" The line went dead.

He had hung up on her! With trembling fingers, she

replaced the receiver. She hadn't even had a chance to explain to him that she wasn't going out with Cal!

When Nora and Frank asked her to go with them to an open house at Timmy's school, she declined. It wasn't that she didn't want to go, because she knew it would be a precious experience to visit the classroom and watch Timmy introduce his parents to his teacher. But she couldn't help but think that Aaron might call back; that he would apologize for hanging up on her; that he would give her a chance to explain.

A half hour after the McKenzie's left, Bethany restlessly turned on the TV. She switched from one channel to another, and finally settled on the news. When she couldn't listen to anymore world chaos, she got up and turned it off.

She paced the room for a while. Every now and then she would glance at the phone, as though willing it to ring, but it remained silent.

Finally, she slipped into her buckskin jacket and went out for a walk.

The night was cool, but pleasant. The sky was clear and dotted with stars and Bethany thought of Abraham and how the Lord reminded him that if He could create and maintain all those stars, He would have no trouble at all in keeping His promise that Abraham would have a son.

How could people look at a sky like that and not believe? she wondered.

When Bethany returned home she heard the phone ringing. Hurriedly, she unlocked the door and ran inside, but when she picked up the receiver, all she heard was a dial tone.

It had to have been Aaron. Bethany quickly lifted

135

the receiver and started to dial his number, then hung up. Would that be wrong for her to do? Would it be presumptuous of her? Suddenly abandoning any concern for caution, she picked up the receiver again, dialing his number. The phone rang and she waited. It continued to ring.

There was no answer.

Thursday morning she borrowed Nora's car and drove to the studio. Cal was busy with another writer and would be tied up the rest of the week. He had told her he wouldn't be able to visit the set of "Agape, John" until the first part of the following week.

Bethany had to see Aaron. She simply had to set things straight between them and let him know that his suspicions of Calvin Bruce were unfounded.

They were shooting on the back lot of the studio. The scene was from the Book of the First Epistle of John. But instead of writing the words of love and of warnings on false teachings, Bethany had decided to let the words be spoken by John to an audience of followers who had begun to go astray. A great heresy had sprung up and John saw fit to denounce this false doctrine and to emphasize love for the brethren.

She found a place to sit over to one side, partially hidden from view by lights and reflectors, but close enough to hear Aaron.

Everything was quiet on the set and the cameras were rolling. She could sense a lack of composure in Aaron. When he began to speak the lines, there was a glaring omission of confidence.

"If we say that we have no sin, we deceive ourselves and there is no truth in us. But if we—"

"Cut!"

The director walked over to Aaron and spoke to him quietly. Bethany couldn't hear what he said but Aaron frowned and shrugged. Then the director resumed his place near the cameras and they began again.

"If we say that we have no sin, we deceive ourselves and—"

"Cut!"

Again, the director went to Aaron and said something to him. This time he patted the actor on the shoulder reassuringly before he returned to his place.

Bethany counted the number of takes in that one scene that followed. Seventeen. Seventeen takes and Aaron was never allowed to finish the sentence. Whatever the director wanted from him, Aaron just wasn't giving it, apparently.

Bethany knew what was missing. To her it was obvious. But did the director feel the same thing? Was he too, a Christian? Or was it merely his experience and professionalism that enabled him just to sense when a spoken line wasn't right?

Again she heard, "Quiet on the set! OK, roll 'em! Action!"

From where she was sitting Bethany could feel Aaron's growing tenseness. His voice now had an edge to it that was razor sharp.

"If we say that we have no sin," he began again. Then, before the director could say "Cut!" he literally ripped off the rough-looking tunic he was wearing, thrust it on the ground, and stomped off the set.

Bethany hurried off to find him. She could hear the director giving orders to "wrap it up" since "Mr. Arrogant Steele" would be in no fit mood to shoot the rest of the day.

Aaron was heading back to his dressing room. He stormed into it and slammed the door. Bethany ran up to it and opened the door without knocking.

Aaron was unfastening the girdle around his waist and one dark eyebrow winged upward when he saw her.

"Well! Come on in and shut the door if you don't mind."

Bethany closed the door and stood nervously against it.

He continued working on the fastenings of the girdle until it was undone and he flung it across the room. "I'm going to undress, as you can probably tell. Want to watch?" He shot her a defiant look.

Bethany tried to ignore his terrible mood. "Aaron, wait a moment."

He bent over to unlace one of his sandals. "I didn't expect to see you here. Where's Cal?"

"I didn't come here with Cal."

"No?"

"No."

He straightened up and kicked the sandal off with asperity. "Well, that's a switch! Did you wear him out last night?"

Before she knew what had happened, the palm of her hand cracked across his handsome cheek, leaving a red mark. Both of them stood motionless for a moment, staring at each other in silence.

Beth's heart pounded. She couldn't believe she had done such a thing! Never in her life had she slapped a man's face!

From the astonished expression he wore, it seemed that Aaron was just as surprised.

"I—I'm really sorry, Aaron. I don't know what came over me. Really!"

He rubbed at his cheek, then grinned. His voice softened. "I needed that, Beth. I really did. I had no right to say that to you. It's just that I'm so jealous of Calvin Bruce, I don't know what to do sometimes."

"But there's no reason to be jealous! None!"

He eyed her shrewdly. "None?"

"No, none."

"He's in love with you, you know!"

"Oh, for heaven's sake! That's nonsense!"

"No, it isn't nonsense, Beth. It's very plain to see that he is."

"Cal is—he's just a good friend. And he's my agent. Nothing more."

"You're sure about that?"

"I'm sure. And I didn't go out with him last night."

"But you said—"

"What I said was that he asked me to go out. But I declined."

"You weren't home, though."

"Yes, I was."

"Don't lie to me. I called and there was no answer."

"I went for a walk. The McKenzie's were at Timmy's school. When I got back the phone was ringing but I was too late in answering it."

He stared at her unbelievingly.

"It was about eight o'clock. Was that you?"

"Yes."

"I tried to call you back but there was no answer."

"I was calling you from a restaurant. I don't know why, really. I presumed you'd be out with Cal, then when I was having dinner, I thought there might be a chance you didn't go after all. But when you didn't answer the phone—"

"Oh, Aaron! What a mix-up!"

He closed the space between them and took her into his arms. "Bethany!" he whispered.

"It's awful when things get all twisted up like that, isn't it, Aaron?"

"Yes. And it's no wonder I couldn't say my lines today. All I could think of was you and Cal."

"You believe me now, don't you? That there's nothing between us?" she asked.

"Yes, honey. I believe you."

"How—how's your cheek?"

He laughed. "It stings! Last time I had my face slapped was in a film four years ago when an actress got carried away and really connected. She wasn't supposed to actually hit me, but she did. She had just had a fight with her boyfriend and for a minute, I believe she thought I was him! Anyway, she nearly broke my jaw!"

"I'm so sorry I did that, Aaron!"

"I know you are, but I really deserved it, Beth." He released his hold on her. "Sit down, honey." His face grew serious.

Bethany sat down and smiled at him adoringly. He looked almost comical with his loose-fitting undertunic and wearing only one sandal, but he was still handsome. The love that filled her heart for Aaron Steele was almost overpowering.

"What am I doing wrong?" he asked.

"In what, Aaron?"

"In that scene. I know my mind wasn't on the lines today but there's something else, isn't there?"

"Yes."

"What? What's missing, Beth?"

"Jesus."

He looked at her in puzzlement a moment. Then he waved a careless hand. "Come on, Beth. Be serious."

"I am serious."

"I need your help, Beth."

"You need His help. You need to take that step, Aaron. Just turn your life over to Him."

He looked down at his feet and wiggled the toes of his bare foot unconsciously. "I'll work on it," he said. Then he looked up at her again and smiled. "Let's go to dinner, Saturday, shall we?"

"Yes."

"I'd ask you out tomorrow only it's my dad's birthday."

"Saturday's fine. I'd love it."

"I'll call you Saturday morning," he said.

"OK." She got up to leave.

"Beth?"

"Yes?"

"I think I'm falling in love with you."

CHAPTER 10

HAVING TO CONCENTRATE ON her writing presented a nearly insurmountable burden. Bethany's heart wanted to sing. She wanted to literally climb on the roof of the house and shout to anyone that would hear, that Aaron Steele was falling in love with her!

Yet, she knew she had to devote the entire day Friday to working on the new play. She had lost too much time as it was, for one reason or another.

The studio was apparently shooting around Aaron today, she reasoned, since he planned to spend the day and evening with his parents.

Adoringly, she thought of him spending time with his family, and for a while she stared out the window, absorbed in daydreams, until she heard the front door close, which jolted her from her reverie.

It was Nora who had just come home from a doctor's appointment. When Bethany had expressed concern earlier about Nora having to go to the doctor, Nora had shrugged it off as "merely a routine exam."

Now, however, the glowing look on Nora's face told Bethany something entirely different.

"It's just as I suspected," she told Bethany. "I'm three month's pregnant!"

"Nora! How wonderful! And you said the doctor's visit was just routine!"

Nora laughed. "I thought you'd be suspecting something since I haven't eaten breakfast with the rest of you for about two weeks now!"

"Well, now that you mention it, I did think it a little odd at first. But I just reasoned that you probably wanted to eat later on, when it was quieter around the house!"

"No, it's that I'm afraid I haven't been able to keep anything down! But the doctor gave me a prescription for the nausea, so hopefully, that will be under control soon!"

Bethany gave Nora a hug. "I'm so happy for you! Does Frank know?"

"I haven't told him the doctor confirmed it, but he was about as certain as I was!" she said. "That old morning sickness is a dead giveaway!"

Nora's joyful news reinforced Bethany's complacency. She returned to her work with a satisfied grin and a mental picture of Aaron as a new father, lovingly and proudly holding their very own baby. How very happy and proud she would be to have his child. How blessed. They would raise that child in the love of Jesus.

She thought of her parents and how thrilled they would be, and she remembered once, how her mother had expressed a longing for grandchildren.

Bethany hadn't thought, at that time, that she would ever fulfill her mother's wish. She was deeply involved in her writing, and no man had ever made enough of an impression on her that she even considered getting married and having his child.

Not until Aaron Steele.

She sighed. She was really jumping the gun. She had to put forth a concentrated effort to push these thoughts from her mind so she could continue with her work.

Around midafternoon, Bethany was really into her writing. So much so, that Nora had to tell her twice that Calvin Bruce was on the phone.

"Hi, Cal!" she said with enthusiasm. "How's it going?"

"Good," he said. "Real good!" She could hear him draw on his cigarette. "You sound all bubbly. Got some good news I ought to know about?"

"Well . . ." She hesitated. It would be presumptuous of her to tell him Nora's good news before Frank was even informed. And she certainly wasn't going to confide in Cal about Aaron's confession of love, and invite more of Calvin's admonitions. "I've really been on a roll today," she said, "with the new play."

"That's great! About time, isn't it?" he teased.

"I suppose you're right!"

"Well, I'm glad to hear it. And—I have some good news, too!"

"You have? What?"

"I'd rather tell you in person. How about dinner tonight? Can you make it?"

"Yes, I sure can. What time?"

"About seven-thirty, OK?"

"Fine, Cal. I'll look forward to it."

When she hung up the phone, she had questions on

her mind as to whether or not she should tell him about Aaron. Perhaps it would be best to wait a while, until there was more tangible evidence. After all, Aaron only said he "thought" he was falling in love with her. It could turn out that he was mistaken, not that she wanted to even consider such a possibility.

Whatever Cal had to report, it certainly must be exhilarating. If it were possible for a man to look radiant, then Calvin Bruce looked just that.

Bethany commented on his light weight sport coat since the weather had turned chilly again. "Will you be warm enough, Cal? It's really getting cold out."

"Maybe not," he said with a shrug, as though he didn't care.

"I don't want you to catch cold."

"I probably won't." He was still smiling.

Bethany was baffled. Whatever it was, he was in some other world, it seemed. "Cal, did you hear what I said? About your coat?"

"Hm? Oh sure!"

When they got in the car, he spread out his hands. "Notice anything different?" he asked with a wide grin.

Bethany stared at his hands in puzzlement. Was that ring he was wearing on his little finger new? No, she was certain it was there before, because she remembered admiring the size of the diamond.

"I—I don't think—"

He interrupted. "Something's missing! Give up?"

"I guess so—what is it?"

"No cigarette between my fingers! I've quit smoking!"

"Really?"

"Yep! Had my last cigarette this afternoon when I was talking to you on the phone."

"But—isn't that a little early to—I mean, it's only been a few hours—"

"No, No! I've really quit, Beth! I have an incentive!"

"An incentive?"

"That's part of the good news!" He started the ignition. "If you don't mind, I think I will just stop by my house and change coats after all," he said. "It'll only take a minute. OK with you?"

"Oh, sure. I think that's a good idea. The temperature really has dropped today."

"Yeah. It's hard for me to notice things like that!" he said with another grin.

"Cal, if I didn't know better, I'd say you were acting like a man in love!"

He eyed her sagaciously. "Think so?"

"Cal! Are you? In love?"

He nodded like a little boy. "I think I am. It's all happened so fast I can't believe it. I keep waiting for my bubble to burst!"

"Well, for heaven's sake! When did all this happen?"

"Remember the other night when I asked you to go to a concert and you couldn't go?"

"Yes."

"Well, I went alone. And I sat next to this really nice lady—her name is Rose—and we talked and I found out she's a writer—and a very good one too, I might add—and it all just took off from there. She's almost my age and divorced and hates cigarette smoking and of course, that's why I have to stop." He laughed. "Does any of that make sense?"

"Some of it, I think!" She laughed at the way he was jabbering. She had never seen Cal so bubbly and almost rattled.

He went on to describe Rose in detail, both in physical appearance and in personality. When he pulled up in front of his house, he added, "I'll tell you all about her at dinner."

Bethany had to suppress a giggle as she couldn't imagine he had left out anything.

"Come on in for a minute," he said, as he opened the door for her. "Tell me if you think my place is suitable."

"Suitable for what?"

"For Rose. I want to ask her for dinner but I just don't know if my house looks good enough," he said. "I need a female opinion."

She grinned. "OK, let's have a look!"

Calvin underestimated the appearance of his house. It was in excellent taste. Though the furniture was old it appeared to either have been taken care of with extreme care, or redone completely, and there was an ample amount of antiques as well.

"It's old stuff," he said, with a sweep of his arm. "But it's comfortable. Most of it belonged to my mother, since my ex-wife cleaned me out of what we had. Other things I've picked up in antique stores and at auctions, or one thing or another. Is it OK, do you think?"

"I love it, Cal."

"You're not just saying that?"

"No, I'm not just saying that. I mean it, it's lovely. I've always admired old furniture and antiques."

"They don't make it like they used to," he said with pride as he patted the back of the sofa.

Her eyes caught sight of a framed mirror and she went closer to examine it. It consisted of two panels of glass, one above the other, and on the upper panel was painted a ship.

"That's quite old," he said. "It belonged to my grandparents, I think. One antique dealer said the ship is supposed to be the Constitution, a vessel that gained fame during the War of 1812. I believe it was a pretty popular subject then, for this type of mirror."

"It's lovely," she said.

From the mirror, she admired other things. A colorful glass paperweight caught her eye and Cal told her it was call "millefiori," which came from the Italian for "a thousand flowers." The style, he explained, was perfected by the Venetians, but copied in other countries. It was fascinating to Bethany that the "millefiori" appeared different as she looked at it from various angles.

"The mustache cup there," Cal said, pointing to a china cup with *Father* lettered in gilt on one side, "belonged to my grandfather."

"I've heard about those."

He laughed. "Funny-looking thing, isn't it? But those old handle-bar moustaches had to be protected. The cup permitted grandfather to sip his coffee or tea without letting his moustache touch the liquid."

And so it went. A pair of dainty pressed-glass slippers, a small pewter teapot, antique brass candlesticks. And Cal seemed to have a lengthy but fascinating story to tell about each one.

He finally looked at his watch. "Good night!" he said in alarm. "We've talked about antiques for an hour and a half. I'll bet you're starved."

She smiled. "I guess I am. I almost forgot about

dinner, and I certainly did forget about the time. I feel like I've just been on a guided tour of some old, historical mansion!''

He grinned. "That's good. I guess you approve then? Of my place, I mean?''

"Oh, certainly!''

"And Rose? Do you think—''

"Rose will be just as fascinated as I was, you can be sure of that!''

He quickly changed into a warmer coat and they left. Just as they got into his car, another vehicle drove slowly by, and Bethany caught her breath. For a moment, she was almost certain the other car belonged to Vivian Gordon. Then she dismissed the idea as being too ridiculous. She had to stop being so jumpy about the actress. She was beginning to see Vivian Gordons behind every bush!

Saturday morning passed slowly. The phone rang a number of times but the calls were all for either Frank or Nora.

Didn't Aaron say he would call her Saturday morning? She was certain he had.

Early in the afternoon she tried to call his house but there was no answer. Perhaps he decided not to call her beforehand. Maybe he would just be by at the usual time to pick her up. Early in the evening she dressed and waited.

But Aaron never came by for her, and he didn't call her.

At eleven o'clock Bethany went to bed, completely baffled, disappointed, and with a heavy heart.

The first person Bethany saw on the set Monday morning was Vivian. The actress fairly slithered over to where Bethany was standing, her sultry eyes gleaming with malevolence.

"Oh hello, Bethany! So nice to see you!"

Bethany was immediately on guard. This was the first time Vivian had shown any signs of being amicable toward her, and she backed up a step or two, almost expecting a Judas kiss to follow.

"Aaron's dressing," Vivian said. "I just came from his dressing room. He'll be along in a minute." She stared at Bethany, probably to see what effect her announcement of having just been in Aaron's dressing room had on her audience.

Bethany remained outwardly unmoved by the news, silently praying that God would give her the strength to endure a conversation with Vivian Gordon, and that she would not say the wrong thing.

"Aaron's such a darling," the actress gushed. "He and I are really close, you know."

Bethany managed a half-smile, hoping that the trembling she felt inside didn't show on the outside.

"I've been to his house so much lately," Vivian went on, "that I feel like I live there!" She touched the long strands of artificial hair that makeup had given her. "I've been with him almost every night."

"Helping him with his lines, I understand," a masculine voice interrupted.

Vivian's eyes narrowed as Cal walked over to stand beside Bethany. "Well," she said, "that's not all we did."

"That's not what Aaron told me," Cal replied. "He said you were helping him with his lines because Beth didn't feel comfortable being alone with him in his house!" His look defied an answer from Vivian. "He also said you didn't like being around his cat!"

Bethany spoke up excitedly. "Oh, he did keep the cat, then?"

Cal grinned. "I don't know what you mean, honey, but he has a cat, I know that." Then he turned back to Vivian who was obviously struggling to find something to say. "Well, Vivian?"

"I—I don't like cats that much," she stammered.

"That's strange," Cal said. "You're so feline yourself, I would think you and cats would hit it off famously!"

"Really, Cal!" she spat out. "I just put up with the animal to be alone with Aaron. Being alone with him is second nature to me!" She turned and left before any response was voiced.

Cal clenched his teeth. "I've just about had it with that woman!" he said.

"Don't blame her, Cal. She's just infatuated with Aaron, that's all."

He looked at her with concern. "And you, Beth? You're pretty crazy about him too, aren't you?"

Bethany turned her head a little. She certainly didn't want tears to rise up in her eyes. Inside she felt more than love for Aaron Steele at the moment. She felt confusion, hurt, and even doubt. The things Vivian said, combined with Aaron's absence Saturday night and the fact that he hadn't called her to explain, all were beginning to weigh heavily on her.

"What about you, Cal?" she asked quickly, hoping to divert his attention from the subject of Aaron Steele. "How are things going with you and Rose?"

His face immediately brightened. "Great!" he exclaimed.

"Did you have her over for dinner yet?"

"Yes, I did. Saturday night!"

"And?"

"And you were right. She loved the place just like you said she would!"

"See? What did I tell you?"

He grinned. "She loves antiques. Isn't that great?"

"Yes, of course it is! I'm happy for you!"

"And Beth, say one of your magic little prayers for me, will you?"

"There's nothing magical about prayer, Cal. But yes, of course I will! What about?"

"I'm seriously thinking of asking Rose to marry me. What do you think of that?"

She threw her arms around his neck and kissed him on the cheek. "Cal. I think that's wonderful!"

He hugged her tightly. "Honey," he said, "I'm sure glad I'm more than just your agent!"

Bethany opened her eyes and her smile faded. Shadowed by a nearby backdrop and intently watching everything that was going on between her and Cal, was Aaron Steele.

The moment their eyes met, Aaron left.

Bethany's heart sank and she pulled loose from Calvin's arms. "Uh—excuse me, will you Cal? I just saw Aaron and I have to—"

He grinned. "Sure, honey. I understand. Go right along!"

She hurried off in the direction she saw Aaron go, being careful not to trip over the cables on the floor or to bump into any other equipment along the way.

His tall figure disappeared around the corner of his dressing room.

"Aaron, wait!" she called. Rounding the corner, she stopped abruptly as she saw him leaning against the door of his dressing room, arms folded across his chest.

He was scowling at her. "Come inside, Beth. I believe we have some serious talking to do," he said.

She went in meekly and sat down when he pointed to a chair.

He towered above her. For a few minutes he just stared at her, and said nothing. The anger in his eyes flashed ominous warnings to Bethany, cautioning her to be prepared for an outburst of rage unlike any she had ever seen.

"I know a lot of disgusting words," he spat out at last, "but in all honesty, I can't think of any that are bad enough to express my feelings toward you at this moment!"

Bethany's heart was pounding. "Aaron, what you just saw between Cal and me—"

"What I saw? What I *saw?*" he yelled. "How about what I *heard?* How about Cal telling you he was glad to be *more* to you than your agent? Explain that, Sweetheart!"

"Aaron, it's—"

"You *can't*, can you? You can't explain it to be any different than what I heard, because it isn't any different!"

Her hands were shaking. Her whole body trembled. And her voice shook as she spoke. "Please, Aaron!"

"Please?"

She swallowed hard. "You have to let me explain!"

"There's nothing to explain! Anything you would say to me now would be lies!"

"No! Listen to me!"

"No, you listen to *me!* I thought I was falling in love with you, Beth. I really did. I thought you were different. Now I know the truth!"

Nausea was churning in her stomach. Was she dreaming this? She tried her best to convince herself it was only a terrible nightmare, but it was useless. Standing before her was the man she loved with all her heart, verbally ripping her into sheds. When she spoke again, her voice was barely above a whisper. "Aaron, you couldn't be farther from the truth!"

"Truth? You're sitting there telling me about *truth?*"

"Aaron—"

"Please, Beth. Just go. Leave me alone. Just leave me alone."

"Not until I make you understand! You couldn't have heard all the conversation when Vivian was there—"

"Vivian was the one who told me where to find you. You and Cal."

Bethany could feel the tears rising in her throat. "Vivian was telling me about going to your house and Cal intervened to explain that it was to help you with your lines."

"That's right. She did. And all because you refused to step foot in my house."

"You know the reason for that, Aaron! I told you—"

"Sure, you told me." A sarcastic laugh followed. "I believed you, too. For awhile."

"But we had a date on Saturday, Aaron. I—I don't understand—"

"You don't?"

"No! Aaron, please—"

154

He pulled her to her feet and pushed her toward the door. "You wouldn't come to my place but you would spend an hour and a half at Calvin Bruce's house with him!"

Bethany's jaw dropped in shock. "That's not . . ." She stopped. She was about to say it wasn't true but it was true. It was all too true. She had been with Cal in his house for that long on Friday night.

Vivian! That must have been Vivian's car she thought she saw when they left! No wonder Aaron hadn't called her on Saturday!

Tears now filled her eyes and rolled down her cheeks. "I know it sounds like something else, Aaron, but it's not! It's . . . it's . . ." Her voice broke into sobs. "Please! You—you have to listen to me. . . ."

He opened the door and his eyes were cold and filled with disgust. "Just leave me alone, Beth." He took her arm, led her outside, and closed the door.

Everything was a blur of tears. Bethany's head was spinning, her stomach churning, her heart pounding. She desperately wished she could just wake up from this horrible dream but she knew she couldn't. It was not a dream. Aaron Steele, the man she loved, believed the absolute worst about her.

Stumbling over the cables, she made her way to a quiet corner of the stage out of sight where she could think. And then she would just call a taxi and go home. When Nora dropped her off at the studio earlier and said she would pick her up later in the afternoon, Beth had expected to stay. She had planned to be with Aaron—to find out why he hadn't called her or seen her Saturday night. Now she knew.

Vivian! Vivian Gordon was responsible for all of this!

155

She sat down on a deserted bench in the half-light and bowed her head. "Oh, dear, sweet Jesus!" she whispered. "Please help me! Help me convince Aaron of the truth!"

A shuffling noise near her made her open her eyes. Looking up through her tears, she gazed upon the face of a man. He was robed in white and a gentle smile was on his bearded face.

"J—Jesus?" she stammered.

"Oh, thank you for the compliment, Beth! No, I'm afraid not! Far from it!" It was Glenn Davidson.

"Oh, Glenn! How silly of me! I . . ."

He sat down next to her. "I'm flattered that I look the part so much." He took her hand and held it gently. "I heard crying. What is it, Beth?"

His tender and sympathetic manner only made her cry all the more, and she gave into the tears for a moment or two before she brought them under control.

"Have a fight with Aaron?" he asked perceptively.

"Yes! It was awful! He—he thinks Cal and I—"

"Oh, no! But Calvin's almost engaged to a woman named Rose, isn't he?"

She nodded. "I didn't even have the chance to tell him that!"

"How come?"

"Well, Cal was telling me that he was going to ask Rose to marry him and I was so pleased for him I gave him a hug. Cal said something about being happy to be more than my agent and he *meant* that he was happy we were such good friends and that I cared about him and Rose—you know."

"Yes, I understand. And?"

"And Aaron heard him say that and gave it a whole different meaning."

"He just happened by when Cal said that to you?"

"Well yes, sort of. Vivian told him—"

"Vivian? Oh, dear! That's a whole new ball game!"

"What do you mean?"

"Vivian's poison, Beth. She can really cause trouble when someone is after a man she wants. And of course, everybody knows she wants Aaron Steele."

Bethany hung her head. "Yes, I know."

He patted her on the arm and stood up. "Did you bring your car?"

"No, Nora brought me. I was going to spend the day, but—"

"Want to leave?"

"Yes. I was just going to call a taxi."

"No need for that. I'm through shooting for the day. You just sit tight, and I'll change my clothes and be right back. We'll go have lunch somewhere and have a nice talk, OK?"

She smiled. "Yes. Thanks, Glenn."

Glenn took her to a well known Japanese restaurant, and at his request, the hostess led them to a private *Tatami* room behind sliding paper-covered doors. Since Bethany had never tasted Japanese food before, Glenn ordered for them both. Soon the waitress had placed in front of them a sizzling platter of shrimp and vegetable tempura, a steaming bowl of rice, and a fresh pot of hot tea.

When the waitress left them alone once more, Glenn bowed his head and offered thanks, and Bethany experienced a peaceful feeling in sitting on the floor, across the table from a brother-in-Christ.

"Now then," he began. "What has Vivian done so far to your relationship with Aaron?"

"Everything possible," Bethany replied, taking a bite of the delicious shrimp.

"Here," Glenn said, placing another piece of tempura on her plate. "That's some zucchini. You must try that—it's terrific." He poured tea into the tiny cups. "Such as?"

"Oh, that zucchini is good!" Bethany exclaimed. "Such as reporting to Aaron that I was sitting next to Cal at the beach, having a good old time."

He nodded. "Sounds like her. What else?"

"Well, that thing about telling Aaron where to find Cal and me this morning. And she's forever trying to impress me with the fact that she and Aaron are really close."

"Lies."

"What?"

"That's a pack of lies. Aaron has no use for Vivian Gordon."

"I wish he'd tell me that."

"You should know it, Beth."

"How?"

"By the way he looks at you. He's in love with you."

She vented a deep sigh. "Well, if he was, he certainly isn't now."

"Oh, come on! Where's your faith?"

"Dragging a bit, I guess."

"Here, have some more rice."

"No, thanks. I'm getting full."

"Already? Look at all that's left!"

"I know. It's really delicious. I'm sorry."

"Don't be. I'm sure I can pack it away. Does that disgust you?" he asked with a grin.

"What? That you have a good appetite? Not at all! You're a big man!"

He sighed. "'Fraid so. I almost missed out on this part because of it!"

"Well, I'm glad you didn't. I think you're perfect for the part. I always picture Jesus as being a bigger and stronger man than is usually portrayed. Maybe that's because I can't remember seeing many carpenters that look frail!"

"Good point!" He refilled their tea cups. "Let's get back to Vivian. Anything else?"

"Friday night she must have followed me."

"What?"

"Aaron spent the day and evening Friday with his family because it was his father's birthday. So when Cal called and asked me to dinner to share his good news, I accepted." She paused. "Was that wrong?"

He shrugged. "Knowing how jealous Aaron seems to be of Cal, probably. But go on."

"Well, we stopped at Cal's house for him to change his coat because it was getting too cold for the one he was wearing. He asked me to come in a minute to look at his house and tell him if I thought it was suitable for him to show to Rose."

He grinned. "Old Cal sure has fallen! And did you?"

"Yes. I didn't think anything of it and neither did Cal. But we got to talking and he told me so many interesting stories about various antiques he has and—well, we were in there a long time."

"How long?"

"Too long. An hour and a half."

He have a low whistle. "Oh, boy!"

"I know. It wasn't right, but God knows I didn't do anything wrong!"

"I know that. What about Vivian?"

"I thought I saw her car when we left his house, but I dismissed it as being my imagination. Now I know it was her car because Aaron knew I was in Cal's house for one and a half hours! She must have told him!"

"Oh, dear! She's worse than I thought! Well, as an old comedian used to say, 'It's a pretty fine mess you've gotten into!'"

"You're right." She took a sip of tea. "What'll I do?"

"We'll pray, first of all. And then, I'll help all I can. Aaron may not believe anything I tell him, but I think he'll listen to Cal. As soon as he knows about Rose, things should straighten out. And Beth, if anything ever happens that you want to pray about, call me, OK? You can always count on me for that!"

Her eyes misted. "Thanks, Glenn," she said in a husky voice. "And—what about Vivian?"

"We'll pray about her, too," he said.

CHAPTER 11

IN SPITE OF THE agonizing torment Bethany had gone through that morning, she felt a sense of peace and well-being when she returned to the house. Having spent time with Glenn Davidson, praying with him and sharing her problems with him, had really helped ease some of the pain she had been feeling.

Nora was in the kitchen when Bethany walked in. "Oh, Beth!" she said in surprise. "I thought you were going to spend the day?"

"No, I—decided not to."

Nora stopped what she was doing and stood motionless, potato peeler in one hand and a half-peeled potato in the other. "Something's wrong. What is it, Beth?"

Bethany sat down in a slump at the kitchen table and Nora quickly poured her a cup of coffee as though the steaming hot beverage would chase away all her ills.

"It's—Aaron," she said, trying to make her voice

sound light. "We had a little misunderstanding, but it will all straighten out." She didn't want to reveal the alarming details of what had happened earlier because of Nora's condition.

"What kind of a misunderstanding?" Nora persisted.

Bethany waved a careless hand and managed a little laugh. "Oh, a silly one. You know how jealous he is of Cal! But as soon as he finds out about Cal's new romance, he'll understand!"

"Cal? In love? When did this happen?"

Bethany was thankful for the distraction from Aaron. She proceeded to tell Nora all about Calvin falling in love.

"Cal needs someone," Nora said. "I'm sure happy to hear that."

"Me, too."

"Here," she said. "Speaking of being in love, have a piece of candy!"

Bethany admired the lovely heart-shaped box of chocolates. "How pretty! That's right, tomorrow is Valentine's Day, isn't it?"

"Yes, and that sweet man of mine had to go and buy me candy!" she said with a pretended sigh of exasperation. "I'll be good and fat soon enough without this! But I'll eat it anyway!" she said good naturedly, popping a chocolate into her mouth. "I love chocolate and he knows it, bless his heart!"

Bethany laughed and helped herself to a cream-filled piece of candy.

She couldn't help but admire the way Nora looked lately. The pregnancy was certainly flattering to the woman, making her skin glow and her eyes sparkle. Of course, being in love did that too, she reasoned. Being happily in love.

She thought of Aaron and how dear it would be if God blessed them with marriage and children. She pictured herself carrying his child, radiant and contented and filled with adoration for her beloved. A touch of melancholy washed over her again, and she wondered what Aaron was doing at this very moment.

"I'm going to go visit Judy right after dinner," Nora said. "Want to come along?"

Bethany quickly considered that being there with the young blind woman and Nora would not be a very good idea. Surely Judy, with her keen sense of perception, would feel Bethany's sadness and comment on it. Then Nora would question her further and she didn't want that.

"I don't think I'd better," she replied. "I've lots of work to do." That was the truth, she thought. She did have a great deal to do on the new play as Cal said he wanted to see and outline before long to show to Mike Innis, and there were a few scenes that Bethany hadn't worked out yet in her mind. She frowned to herself, realizing that she was losing some of the discipline in her writing schedule so she excused herself to get to work.

It was well into the evening when the phone rang. Since Frank had taken Timmy roller skating and Nora had gone to visit with Judy, Bethany was alone in the house and she had to run to answer it.

"Bethany! How are you?"

The acrid voice of Vivian Gordon startled her. What possible reason could the actress have for calling?

"Vivian?"

"Yes! You may be wondering why I called."

"Well, yes—"

"I just wanted to apologize for getting so upset today at the studio."

"Apologize?"

"Yes. But then, Calvin has a way of upsetting me, sometimes. But I shouldn't say anything about him that isn't nice. I mean, I know you're a little prejudiced where he's concerned!"

"Vivian, you don't seem to understand—"

"But that's nice, Bethany," she interrupted. "He's a good person, I suppose. Oh, did I tell you what a wonderful time I had with Aaron Friday when he took me to meet his parents?"

Bethany's heart felt as though someone had pounded it flat. "Pardon me?"

"Oh, I guess he didn't tell you! Naughty boy! Well, anyway, I just wanted to call to say I was sorry for the way I acted toward you and Cal today. I have to go now, Bethany. Someone's at my front door. Bye!"

Bethany replaced the receiver in shock. The news that Aaron had taken Vivian to meet his parents went through her like a shockwave. To think that he shared that precious family day with Vivian Gordon!

She started crying before she knew what was happening, and for a few minutes her tears were uncontrollable. She simply surrendered to the crushing news as though nothing else mattered. Then she stopped, remembering that the Lord told her to "stand still and wait." Certainly He didn't intend for her to fall apart over some obstacle. He could remove that obstacle! She could only see the miserable present, but He could see way ahead. She had to remember that.

She felt like praying with someone, but even if Nora

and Frank were home, she wouldn't want to burden them with this. Not now.

Suddenly, she thought of Glenn Davidson. Glenn had offered to pray with her any time and especially now, with Vivian so involved, he would be more than willing. She dialed his number.

"Glenn? It's Bethany."

"Oh, hi! How are things going?"

"Well I—when you told me today you'd pray with me any time, I'll bet you didn't think it would be so soon, did you?"

His voice became serious. "I'll be right over."

"Really?"

"Sure! We'll go somewhere for coffee, OK?"

"That sounds good."

"I'll be there in a few minutes."

"OK. Thanks, Glenn."

Glenn took her to a small, rather intimate coffee shop near the beach. It was filled with healthy, thriving plants, and the ceiling was draped with swags of colorful, printed cotton cloth. The waitress had on a mid-calf-length skirt and sandals and wore her long hair in braids. She seated them in a secluded corner booth.

Glenn studied the menu. "Um—avocado and sprouts and cream cheese on a whole wheat bun. Doesn't that sound good?"

"Didn't you eat dinner?"

"Oh, sure! But just a sandwich—how about it? Are you hungry?"

Bethany smiled at his never-ending appetite. "Don't you ever fill up?" she asked jokingly.

"No, I don't think so."

She laughed. "Well, I did have dinner, thank you. And I'm not hungry. But I will have a cup of herb tea and a bran muffin to keep you company!"

When the waitress took their order and left, he became serious again. "What happened?" he asked.

Bethany could feel a lump rising in her throat again and she swallowed hard before answering. "Viv—Vivian called me."

"She called *you?*"

"She said it was to apologize for getting so upset at the studio today with me and Cal."

"Apologize? Vivian? Well, I hope God forgives me, but that's hard to believe."

"Well, she had another reason for calling, it seems."

"I'll bet. What was it?"

"She just casually told me that she went with Aaron Friday to meet his parents!"

"Oh, come on! That doesn't make sense! I just can't believe Aaron would do that."

"Well, he did. And you know what that means!"

"What does it mean?"

"Glenn! When a man takes a girl home to meet his family, it means he's in love with her and wants to marry her."

"Who says?"

"Everybody says! It's just done that way!"

"Sounds kind of old-fashioned to me, Beth. But then, I don't know much about those things. My parents died when I was little."

"I'm sorry."

"No, don't be. That's beside the point, anyway. I just can't imagine Aaron wanting Vivian Gordon to meet his family! If he were going to take anyone to meet them, I would say it would have to be you."

"Oh, Glenn! Will you pray for me?"

"Of course I will. Let's pray right now." He reached across the table for her hand and paused a moment before he began. "Lord, we come before You now because we are in agreement and claiming the Scripture that 'all things work together for good to them that love God.' And Lord, You know how much we both love You. . . ."

Tears filled her eyes as Glenn softly prayed. It was not a lengthy prayer and it was simple. Yet it was from the heart and at his "Amen" Bethany drew a deep breath of relief.

"Thanks, Glenn."

"Any time, Beth. I told you that."

"I feel better already."

"Of course you do. So do I," he said. "Wait a minute!"

"What?"

"Praise the Lord!"

"What?"

"She lied to you, Beth."

"Who? Vivian?"

"Yes. She never went to meet Aaron's family at all."

"How do you know?"

"Didn't you tell me that Aaron said he would be gone Friday evening as well and that's why you went to dinner with Cal?"

"Yes, but—"

"Don't you see? Vivian couldn't have gone with him."

"I don't understand. Why not?"

"Because she was too busy spying on you and Cal."

"You're right!" The sudden elation Glenn's reasoning offered her was exhilarating. "Why didn't I think of that?"

He shrugged. "I don't know. Maybe you're too close to the problem. Anyway, the Lord enlightened us." He looked at her tenderly. "You know, Aaron's a lucky guy to have you."

She blushed. "Well, thank you, but he doesn't 'have' me as you put it. I mean, I don't know what's going to happen, Glenn. He's not a Christian yet, you know."

"I know. But I've a feeling he will be."

"Me, too. I hope it's soon."

"Yes. It makes a difference, doesn't it?"

"What?"

"Being with another Christian. I used to date a lot before I was converted. I'd party and drink like a fish and use a different girl every night. And I mean 'use.' Does that shock you?"

She blushed again. "Well—I suppose. . . . It's just hard to imagine. . . ."

"You've only known me as a Christian, Beth. You should have known me before. I wasn't a very nice person to be around."

"And Jesus changed all that."

"Yes, He did!"

"The trouble is, though, I don't have anyone to date now. The girls I used to go out with don't interest me anymore!"

"You'll meet someone, Glenn."

"Yes, it is important."

The waitress brought their order and Glenn gave thanks and then took a bite of the sandwich. "Um—sure you don't want one of these?" he asked. "It's really delicious!"

168

"No, thank you," she replied. "The muffin and tea will be plenty."

"OK. Well, getting back to what I was saying—I've given it a lot of thought lately. And I'm going to pray about it. I'm going to ask God to send me a Christian woman."

"That's wonderful!"

"Do you think He will?"

"Certainly!"

"Looks aren't important. What I want is a gentle, loving person, who loves me and loves the Lord. And not necessarily in that order!"

"I think God can handle that!"

"And of course, a nice bonus would be that she would enjoy good music and poetry. But the most important thing is that she loves the Lord as much as I do. I don't care if she has two heads!"

Bethany laughed. "I'm sure your prayers will be answered!" She took a sip of tea. "Wait—did you say poetry?"

He shrugged boyishly. "Yes. I don't admit that to many people, but I really like it. I even tried to write some, but I'm not sure how good it is."

"Glenn—tell you what."

"What?"

"As soon as we finish eating, we're going for a short drive."

"We are? Where?"

"Not far from here. There's someone I want you to meet!"

Nora was just leaving Judy's house when Bethany and Glenn drove up. She seemed a little surprised to see them, especially after Bethany had told her how much work she had to do. But she greeted them warmly and then left.

Judy quieted Melvin and asked them inside. "How nice of you to come, Beth!" she said.

"I want you to meet someone, Judy. This is Glenn Davidson."

Glenn extended his hand. "Pleased to meet you," he said. When Judy didn't take his hand, he puzzled, until he realized she was blind. He seemed a little uneasy at first and looked for something to say. Then he spotted the bandage on her foot. "Uh—did you hurt your foot, Judy?" he asked.

"Yes! Stupid of me," she said. "But Beth and Aaron were here and rescued me from my own front porch!" Her laugh was pleasant and Glenn smiled as they sat down.

"Excuse me a minute, and I'll get us some coffee."

Glenn started to get up to help, but Bethany placed a restraining hand on his arm, and smiled. "Coffee sounds good," she said. "Is it made, Judy?"

"Yes. I made a big pot, but Nora didn't want any," she called from the kitchen. "Said coffee tastes terrible! Isn't that wonderful?!"

"Sure is!"

Glenn looked more confused than ever. "What's wonderful about coffee tasting terrible?"

Judy came back into the room, laughing. She placed the tray on the table. "Oh, no! That's funny!" she said. "Don't you know about Nora?"

"Know what?"

"Nora's pregnant," Bethany said. "Isn't that great?"

"Oh, that is good news! Is that why coffee doesn't taste good to her?"

"I guess so!" Bethany turned to Judy. "I see you're not using your crutches."

"Nope! The ankle is healing really well! I'll be good as new, soon!"

"Glad to hear that!"

Judy turned to where she knew Glenn was sitting. "What do you do, Glenn?"

"I'm an actor."

"Oh, really? Goodness! Do you know Aaron Steele, too?"

"Sure do."

"Glenn is going to be in the play I told you about," Bethany said.

"Really? What part do you have, Glenn?"

"I'm going to play Jesus."

When Judy said, "Oh!" it was more like a reverent sigh than an exclamation. "How marvelous!" she whispered. "How blessed to be able to play our precious Savior!"

Glenn's face brightened. "You're a Christian, too?"

"Oh, yes! Yes!"

Glenn studied the girl's lovely face pensively. Though void of sight, Judy's eyes seemed to glow with a special kind of light—of love for her God.

"Oh, and Glenn," Bethany said casually, "You'll probably be interested in the fact that Judy writes poetry. I mean, since you like poetry so much."

Judy leaned forward. "Do you like poetry, Glenn?"

He grinned. "Yes, I really do," he said eagerly. "Could I see some of yours?"

"Well, as I told Beth, I'd rather wait until I've finished a little more. In a couple of days though, I'm expecting someone who types my poems for me from the tape recorder I use. When she finishes, I can let you see them, if that's OK."

"Love to. Could I call you?"

"Oh, yes! I'd really like that! Are you sure you want to read them?"

"Very! Are you sure you won't be busy?"

"Oh, I'm never that busy!" She blushed. "What I mean is," she added quickly. "I'm usually home, Glenn."

"I'll give you a call, then!"

When Bethany returned home, the McKenzies had all gone to bed. But even though it was late, she found it easy to return to her work and concentrate on her writing for quite some time.

When she finally pulled herself away from her writing, she reflected on the time spent earlier. It had been a refreshing evening, being with Glenn and Judy.

She didn't know what she had started between the two of them, but even if it only amounted to a good Christian friendship, she knew that was something they both needed.

She thought of Aaron and of the terrible mix-up that had happened. She thought of Vivian Gordon and the woman's obsession to have Aaron Steele, no matter who was hurt in the process. She thought of Calvin Bruce and Rose and how happy she was for them. And she thought of Glenn and what a dear friend he had turned out to be and she thought of Judy—how sweet and gentle the girl was.

Then her jumbled maze of thoughts returned to Aaron. She prayed long and hard abut their friendship. That things would iron out between them and he would understand. And she prayed once more that

God would give Aaron that blessed peace that only comes from Jesus.

As she drifted off to sleep the same peace she had asked for Aaron filled her being and she smiled.

"I'll wait, Lord," she whispered. "But please, help me to be content while I'm waiting!"

CHAPTER 12

HER NIGHT WAS SURPRISINGLY undisturbed, and she thought of the Scripture: "He giveth His beloved sleep."

Bethany's mind had been so cluttered when she went to bed the night before, that she sincerely doubted sleep would come easily. She pictured herself tossing fitfully for half the night, trying to deposit all her assorted thoughts into their respective little compartments and closing the lid on them so she could rest. But God had been gracious as usual and given her a peaceful slumber.

She yawned contentedly and stretched as she made her way into the kitchen.

Nora greeted her cheerfully. "Good morning, sleepy-head! You really must have been tired!"

"I was. Oh, thank you!" Bethany gratefully accepted the mug of hot black coffee.

"That should open your eyes," Nora said with a giggle. "Frank said I made it strong enough to stand alone!"

Bethany yawned again and smiled. "Where are Frank and Timmy?"

"Long gone, kiddo. It's nine-thirty."

Bethany widened her eyes. "Nine-thirty? Oh, my goodness! How did I ever sleep that late? You should have called me!"

Nora shrugged. "I felt you needed the sleep."

"I suppose I did. How do you feel, Nora?"

"You know, I feel great! The pills the doctor gave me really work. I even had a cup of this coffee this morning, and that's the supreme test, believe me!"

Bethany grinned. "Glad to hear that. Judy said you couldn't touch a cup of it last night."

"No way! Her coffee is always good, too. But this morning, I didn't even lose my breakfast!"

Bethany shook her head. "That must be an awful feeling."

Nora smiled and patted her still-flat stomach. "It's worth it!" she said. "Do you want some eggs?"

"No, I'm just going to have a piece of toast. Cal will be here pretty soon, I think, to take me to the studio."

"Big day, today?"

"I guess. I know Glenn has to be there. I forgot to ask him what they're going to do today."

"I was surprised to see you and Glenn at Judy's house last night."

"I'll bet you were. Especially since I had already declined your invitation to go there."

"Oh, it wasn't that. Anyone can change their mind. Besides, Beth, I was glad to see you do something besides work for a change!"

Bethany took a bite of toast. "I called Glenn earlier to ask him to pray with me."

Nora quickly sat down, her face serious. "Beth, what happened?"

Bethany tried to sound as casual as possible. "Nothing monumental, really. Last night I thought so for a while but—"

"Aaron?"

"Well—indirectly. Actually, Vivian called me."

"Vivian Gordon? What did she want?"

"It was all very strange, Nora. She didn't talk very long or say much. It seems her main objective was to inform me that Aaron had taken her to meet his parents."

"His parents? Vivian?" Nora's expression was one of hurt and anger.

"Yes. Well—it was a lie, because Glenn knew she hadn't gone there. Anyway, Glenn took me for a drive to the beach, and we had tea and talked and prayed, and I felt better." She was hoping her explanation would satisfy Nora, since she didn't want to have to go into great detail concerning Vivian's underhanded attempts at spying on her and Cal.

"How come you wound up at Judy's?" she asked.

Bethany grinned. "When Glenn and I were talking he said he was looking for a Christian girl friend."

"And you were playing matchmaker?"

Bethany shrugged. "Not really. He said he liked poetry though, and I thought of Judy and what she said about writing poetry."

"It's beautiful poetry," Nora said. "I've seen some of it."

"You have?"

"Yes. Quite some time ago. She writes Christian poems, mostly free verse."

"Well, Glenn seemed interested."

Nora leaned forward eagerly. "Yes? And how did he like her?"

Bethany stood up and poured herself another cup of coffee, then sat down again, while Nora expectantly waited for an answer.

"He seemed to think she's really nice."

Nora beamed. "Wouldn't that be something? If they hit it off?"

"Sure would. But that really wasn't my intention, Nora."

"Of course it wasn't," she said playfully.

"I mean, if something comes of it, great. But what is most important is that they become friends."

"You're right. That is important. I just have a habit of jumping the gun when it comes to playing cupid!"

"So I've noticed!" They both laughed. "I think Judy could use the friendship of a Christian man," Bethany said. "Not that she hasn't any. I'm sure Frank is a good friend, and there must be others. But Glenn—"

"Is single and available."

Bethany giggled. "Exactly! Anyway, he needs someone, too. He was telling me he doesn't date any more."

"Not at all?"

"Not now. Seems he really was quite a different person before his conversion and the girls he had then were—well, he's just not interested in them any more."

"I can understand that." Nora sighed. "Judy's so sweet. And she's rather pretty, I think. Don't you?"

"Yes, I do. It also amazes me the way she gets around. Has she been blind long?"

"Years. It was an automobile accident when she

was a little girl. Her parents were killed in the accident, and she was raised by an aunt who was a Christian."

"Was?"

"She passed away about three years ago. That's her house Judy lives in. She left it to Judy."

"Oh, I see. No wonder Judy's so used to it."

"I sometimes think Judy can see as much as anyone with sight."

"Maybe more."

"Yes. The Bible speaks so much of spiritual blindness—those that can't or won't see the truth. In that respect, Judy has 20/20 vision!"

"I'll agree to that!"

The doorbell interrupted them and Nora went to answer it. When she brought Calvin Bruce into the kitchen, Bethany flushed.

"Well, look at this!" he said with a wide smile. "I thought you'd be all ready to go!"

She ran her fingers through uncombed hair in embarrassment. "I'm sorry, Cal. I didn't expect you to be here so early."

"Early? It's ten o'clock!"

"Oh. Uh—so it is! Well, I'd better get dressed, then, hadn't I?"

"Not a bad idea!" he said teasingly.

"Sit down, Cal," Nora said, "and I'll feed you some breakfast while you're waiting for Beth."

"Oh, you don't have to." But he sat down at the table anyway. "Maybe just a little bite," he said with a wide grin on his face.

"You're sure in a great mood!" Nora said playfully. "You look like a Cheshire cat! What's gotten into you, Cal?"

He winked at Bethany. "Oh, just happy in love, I guess!" he said, taking a big swallow of coffee.

On the way to the studio, Bethany had to comment on Calvin's enthusiastic mood. "Things must be going really good for you and Rose!" she commented good naturedly.

"They are!"

"Well? For heaven's sake, stop grinning and tell me what's going on!"

He laughed. "I asked her to marry me. And she accepted!"

"Cal! That's wonderful news!"

"That's not all the good news, though."

"What's the rest?"

"You'll find out!"

He whistled the rest of the way, and Bethany could hardly contain her curiosity, but Cal would tell her no more.

When they reached the studio, he took her by the hand and fairly dragged her to the sound stage where they were shooting, "Agape, John."

The minute they went in, she saw Aaron at the other end of the stage. He looked in her direction, then walked toward her and Bethany experienced a curling sensation of fear in her stomach over what he would say upon seeing her and Cal together again.

But her fears were unjustified. As he drew nearer, he broke into a grin, and when he reached them, he actually gave Cal a warm greeting and a friendly pat on the shoulder.

Bewildered, Bethany looked up at him and as he gazed into her eyes she saw no anger, no jealousy, no resentment.

"I'll be back to talk to you as soon as I'm finished," he said. "We have a lot to discuss, Bethany." He returned to the set.

Bethany turned to Cal in puzzlement and he winked at her again. "I don't understand, Cal. . . ."

"It's all fixed," he said.

"What's all fixed?"

"You'll find out."

"*Cal!*"

"Shh!" He put a finger to his lips to silence her as the director called, "Quiet on the set!"

They took a few steps closer to observe. It was the same scene they had tried to shoot a few days before when Aaron couldn't get through his lines and wound up storming off the set.

"Please, God," she prayed silently. "Help him. Help him now."

"OK, action!"

"If we say that we have no sin, we deceive ourselves and the truth is not in us. But if we confess our sins to God, He will forgive us. . . ."

Bethany found herself holding her breath. He got through that line all right, and the director didn't say, "Cut!" And he *did* sound more convincing this time, that was a certainty.

She silently prayed again. "Please God, let him go on and do it well!"

"God is light and there is no darkness in Him."

Bethany's heart stirred. Was there something different in his voice?

"Do not love the world or anything that belongs to the world. . . ."

Bethany glanced at the director to see if he seemed satisfied with what he was hearing and seeing. The man was leaning forward in his chair, a cigar in his mouth. The ashes of the cigar were ready to fall, but he seemed not to notice. He was listening intently. She looked around. Everyone was listening intently.

Aaron's voice became a little softer but it was still very audible. The stillness on the set was simply incredible.

"The world does not know us because it has not known God," he said quietly. "My dear friends, we are now God's children. . . ."

The extras standing around him were serious, listening eagerly. Bethany studied their faces. Either they were all born-again Christians, which was not likely, or they were all excellent actors. Or there was just something that Aaron Steele was sharing with those around him that represented a powerful force. Though he was soft-spoken at the moment, he was talking with incredible authority.

He bent over and picked up two small sticks in the shape of a cross. Then he held it out in front of him and his eyes misted with tears. "This is love," he said softly. "Not that we loved God, but that He loved us and sent His Son as an atoning sacrifice for our sins. Dear friends, since God so loved us, we also ought to love one another." His eyes were glistening. "This—*this* is love!" he said in a voice that broke with emotion.

Tears filled Bethany's eyes. There *was* something different about him. She could feel it. It flowed from his being and through his lines. It filled those around him. It filled the entire stage. It was as though God had poured out His tenderness from a huge heavenly bucket and drenched His audience with love.

Bethany even found it difficult to breathe, so

181

filled—so smothered was she with the presence of God.

When Aaron finished, he stood motionless, breathing heavily. Tears now rolled unashamedly down his cheeks. He seemed both drained and exhilarated.

After what seemed like five more minutes, the director finally said, "Cut! Print it." No one moved. A few minutes passed and the director said, "That's a print." Then the people began to move again from their trancelike state.

Aaron came over to where Bethany was standing and he took her by the arm. "Come over here," he said gently, leading her to a corner of the sound stage. "I need to talk to you."

Bethany followed. She could feel something had happened to him. There was no mistake in that.

His arms closed around her. "Something happened to me just now," he said. "I can't explain it, but I'm not the same person. Does that make any sense at all?"

"Oh, yes!" she cried happily. She was no longer able to control her tears, nor did she care if she did. "Yes, dear Aaron! That's what I've been trying to tell you all along!"

He held her close. "I told my parents about you the other day, Beth. They want to meet you."

"And I want to meet them, too!" Her arms wound around his neck. She couldn't help but feel a twinge of sadness for Vivian, but she couldn't think about that now. She would pray for Vivian, that was a promise she made to God. But at the moment, she didn't care to think about Vivian Gordon.

"Sweetheart, I'm so sorry for the way I acted yesterday."

"I understand. It's OK.'

"No, it isn't OK, Beth. But late last night—very late, I might add—Glenn Davidson came to my house with Cal. I greeted them both with clenched fists for bothering me and Gabriel at that hour."

"Did you say Gabriel?"

"Yes. Oh, you didn't know. I named the cat Gabriel, because he's white and all, and kind of was like an angel in disguise, I think, to open my eyes to the Truth!"

"I think that's a beautiful name! And I'm so happy you kept him!"

"I am too, now. Except that I'm not so sure Gabriel will be a good name."

"Why?"

"I may have to change it to Gabrielle."

"Oh, no!" She laughed. "Maybe one of these days you'll have a lot of little angels running around the house."

"That's what Glenn said," he said with a chuckle. "But I'd better get back to that. At first I was angry that they came over, but I soon changed my tune."

"You did?"

"Yes. I heard all about Rose. Now I know everything! What a knot-head I was!"

"No, you weren't. Just confused. I really understand, Aaron."

"I love you, Beth," he said simply.

Her breath caught in her throat and an overpowering sense of joy filled her. "I love you too," she said.

He kissed her. "I was hoping you'd say that!" he said softly. "Did you get my flowers?"

"Flowers?"

"Oh. I guess you didn't. I told the florist to get

them there early, but this being Valentine's Day and all, I guess they're swamped with orders. Anyway, I sent you some flowers for Valentine's Day."

"You did?"

"Red roses."

"Really? I love roses!"

"And I love you!" He held her tightly. "You will marry me, won't you?" he whispered.

"Yes! Yes, of course I'll marry you!"

"You knew I'd ask?"

"Yes. I just had to stand still and wait!"

He kissed her long and hard. "I think we'd better get married pretty soon, don't you? I'm really not made of steel like some people say I am!"

She blushed and lowered her eyes. "Very soon," she whispered.

They held each other close. This was another kind of love that was real, she thought. Love between a man and a woman. And this was just one of the countless blessings that God, in His Infinite Love, gives His children.

Love is the very nature of God, she thought, and the unity of her and Aaron in marriage would be of God's creative will, for from the Lord would come the love and grace that would enable them to grow together, to raise a family, to share their lives.

Their marriage would be contracted "in the Lord." They would humbly offer thanksgiving and praise for bringing them together.

She would offer to Aaron that precious gift that God had her preserve for him alone. And Aaron would receive that gift, giving to her all of his love in return.

Thinking back, she realized that God knew all along who the man was that she would marry. How beautiful He planned it all! How gently God led Aaron, permitted other Christians to touch his life, planned their meeting, that his heart would be right with Jesus at this point in time, when he asked Bethany to become his wife!

In awe, she looked up adoringly into the face of the man she loved and asked herself a question.

Was there another woman on earth as happy as she was at this very moment?

And when his mouth descended on hers again, she praised God for the answer.

ABOUT THE AUTHOR

CATHIE LeNOIR is an author and music lover. Her background for BORN TO BE ONE grew from study and work with the motion picture industry in California. Cathie says that a bit of herself always appears in her fictional characters. Like her heroine, Bethany, she understands the trials a Christian woman faces in dealing with temptations, in having a close relationship with a non-believer, and in depending on the guidance of the Holy Spirit.

Cathie works as a trust representative for an engineering firm, is the mother of two daughters, and makes her home in Montana.

A Letter To Our Readers

Dear Reader:

Pioneering is an exhilarating experience, filled with opportunities for exploring new frontiers. The Zondervan Corporation is proud to be the first major publisher to launch a series of inspirational romances designed to inspire and uplift as well as to provide wholesome entertainment. In order that we might better contribute to your reading enjoyment, we would appreciate your taking a few minutes to respond to the following questions and return to:

> Editor, Serenade Books
> The Zondervan Publishing House
> 1415 Lake Drive, S.E.
> Grand Rapids, Michigan   49506

1. Did you enjoy reading BORN TO BE ONE?

   ☐ Very much. I would like to see more books by this author!
   ☐ Moderately
   ☐ I would have enjoyed it more if _____

2. Where did you purchase this book? _____

3. What influenced your decision to purchase this book?

   ☐ Cover   ☐ Back cover copy
   ☐ Title   ☐ Friends
   ☐ Publicity   ☐ Other _____

4. Please rate the following elements from 1 (poor) to 10 (superior).

- ☐ Heroine
- ☐ Hero
- ☐ Setting
- ☐ Plot
- ☐ Inspirational theme
- ☐ Secondary characters

5. Which settings would you like to see in future Serenade/Saga Books?

_____ _____

_____ _____

6. What are some inspirational themes you would like to see treated in future books?

_____ _____

_____ _____

7. Would you be interested in reading other Serenade/Serenata or Serenade/Saga Books?

- ☐ Very interested
- ☐ Moderately interested
- ☐ Not interested

8. Please indicate your age range:

- ☐ Under 18
- ☐ 18–24
- ☐ 25–34
- ☐ 35–45
- ☐ 46–55
- ☐ Over 55

9. Would you be interested in a Serenade book club? If so, please give us your name and address:

Name _____

Occupation _____

Address _____

City _____ State _____ Zip _____

Serenade Serenata Books are inspirational romances in contemporary settings, designed to bring you a joyful, heart-lifting reading experience.

Serenade Serenata books available in your local bookstore:

#1   ON WINGS OF LOVE, Elaine L. Schulte
#2   LOVE'S SWEET PROMISE,
       Susan C. Feldhake
#3   FOR LOVE ALONE, Susan C. Feldhake
#4   LOVE'S LATE SPRING, Lydia Heermann
#5   IN COMES LOVE, Mab Graff Hoover
#6   FOUNTAIN OF LOVE, Velma S. Daniels and
       Peggy E. King.
#7   MORNING SONG, Linda Herring
#8   A MOUNTAIN TO STAND STRONG,
       Peggy Darty
#9   LOVE'S PERFECT IMAGE, Judy Baer
#10 SMOKY MOUNTAIN SUNRISE,
       Yvonne Lehman
#11 GREENGOLD AUTUMN,
       Donna Fletcher Crow
#12 IRRESISTIBLE LOVE, Elaine Anne McAvoy
#13 ETERNAL FLAME, Lurlene McDaniel
#14 WINDSONG, Linda Herring
#15 FOREVER EDEN, Barbara Bennett
#16 THE DESIRES OF YOUR HEART,
       Donna Fletcher Crow
#17 CALL OF THE DOVE, Madge Harrah
#18 TENDER ADVERSARY, Judy Baer
#19 HALFWAY TO HEAVEN, Nancy Johanson
#20 HOLD FAST THE DREAM, Lurlene McDaniel
#21 THE DISGUISE OF LOVE, Mary LaPietra
#22 THROUGH A GLASS DARKLY, Sara Mitchell

Serenade Saga Books are inspirational romances in historical settings, designed to bring you a joyful, heart-lifting reading experience.

Serenade Saga books available in your local bookstore:

#1 SUMMER SNOW, Sandy Dengler
#2 CALL HER BLESSED, Jeanette Gilge
#3 INA, Karen Baker Kletzing
#4 JULIANA OF CLOVER HILL,
   Brenda Knight Graham
#5 SONG OF THE NEREIDS, Sandy Dengler
#6 ANNA'S ROCKING CHAIR,
   Elaine Watson
#7 IN LOVE'S OWN TIME,
   Susan C. Feldhake
#8 YANKEE BRIDE, Jane Peart
#9 LIGHT OF MY HEART, Kathleen Karr
#10 LOVE BEYOND SURRENDER,
   Susan C. Feldhake
#11 ALL THE DAYS AFTER SUNDAY,
   Jeanette Gilge
#12 WINTERSPRING, Sandy Dengler
#13 HAND ME DOWN THE DAWN,
   Mary Harwell Sayler
#14 REBEL BRIDE, Jane Peart
#15 SPEAK SOFTLY, LOVE, Kathleen Yapp
#16 FROM THIS DAY FORWARD, Kathleen Karr
#17 THE RIVER BETWEEN, Jacquelyn Cook
#18 VALIANT BRIDE, Jane Peart
#19 WAIT FOR THE SUN, Maryn Langer

Watch for other books in the *Serenade Saga* series coming soon:

#20 KINCAID OF CRIPPLE CREEK, Peggy Darty
#21 LOVE'S GENTLE JOURNEY, Kay Cornelius